CHASE

A SAVAGE KINGS MC NOVEL

LANE HART

D.B. WEST

COPYRIGHT

This book is a work of fiction. The characters, incidents, and dialogue were created from the authors' imagination and are not to be construed as real. Any resemblance to actual people or events is coincidental.

The authors acknowledge the copyrighted and trademarked status of various products within this work of fiction.

Editor's Choice Publishing

P.O. Box 10024

Greensboro, NC 27404

Edited by Angela Snyder
Cover by Marianne Nowicki of PremadeEbookCoverShop.com
Photographer: Dan Ostergren
Cover model: Seth Maras

WARNING: THIS BOOK IS NOT SUITABLE FOR ANYONE UNDER 18. PLEASE NOTE THAT IT CONTAINS EMOTIONAL SCENES THAT MAY BE A TRIGGER FOR INDIVIDUALS WHO HAVE BEEN IN SIMILAR SITUATIONS.

PROLOGUE

Chase Fury

Ten years ago...

"I FUCKING LOVE SEEING MY NAME ON YOUR SKIN," I TELL Sasha. Bringing her wrist up to my lips, I place a kiss just below the small, black cursive letters. While her new tattoo is only a few inches wide, it may as well be the size of a fucking Mack truck for how damn hard my cock is right now, knowing she's mine.

"Good, because it's sort of permanent," Sasha replies with a grin. Her big, blue eyes sparkling up at me from underneath the street-lamps are full of adoration and love that I don't deserve. And God, she's so fucking beautiful it hurts. I was a goner from the second I saw her long, sexy legs and her incredible ass hanging out of her cutoff shorts while she worked under the hood of a 1967 Mustang.

"Permanent is exactly why I like it," I tell her as I wrap my arms around her lean waist to drag her body against mine. She's the tallest woman I know, Cindy Crawford model height, but I still have at least seven inches on her.

Sasha pushes open the leather cut that I'm wearing with no shirt underneath to run her fingernail carefully around my fresh ink — her name that's written in thick, black cursive letters on the left side of my chest.

"My parents are gonna be so pissed when they find out," she says. Her smile grows even wider, which is no surprise. I quickly learned that my girl gets off on excitement and danger, anything that her parents would threaten to whoop her ass over even though she just turned eighteen.

"So, what if they are?" I ask. "They're always pissed at you lately, ever since you started seeing me."

"Very true, it's just..."

When she lowers her eyes and pauses, I grab her chin between my thumb and finger to make her look at me. "Just what?"

"What if it's bad luck?" she asks as her front teeth nervously work over her bottom lip.

"What's bad luck?"

"Doesn't everyone say it's the kiss of death for all relationships if you get your lover's name tattooed on you? I mean, what if my parents are right and we *are* moving too fast, Chase?"

"Shh, calm down baby," I tell her as I grasp her gorgeous, flawless face between both of my palms. "Fast is the only fucking way that I know how to move. And it's *not* bad luck or anything else," I assure her. "That's just a bunch of superstitious bullshit. Because you and me? We're fucking forever, sweetheart. I'm so damn certain of that, I would make you my old lady right now, if I could. I have *zero* fucking doubts that you're the only woman I'll ever want."

"Seriously?" she asks as her eyes start to glisten under the glow of the lights in the parking lot. "You would marry me and give up all the clubhouse sluts?"

"Hell yes," I say without any hesitation. Before Sasha and I got together, I slept with a handful of the girls that hang around the *Savage Asylum*, the bar that also houses the Savage Kings MC's clubhouse. Those women will fuck anything in leather, even prospects like me, still trying to patch in. I haven't touched a single one of them since Sasha and I started seeing each other six months ago. There isn't a girl in that clubhouse that can turn my head. I'm so certain of what we have that I tell Sasha, "Let's do it. Let's get married tonight. We could fly to Vegas..."

"My parents would never –" she starts to say, but my lips crashing down on hers puts a stop to her words.

When I pull back, I look her in the eyes to let her know I'm dead serious. "Fuck what your parents think. Marry me, and then we'll get our own place and they won't be able to say shit about what we do."

Sasha studies my face for several long seconds, judging my sincerity while I hold my breath. Finally, she says, "Okay."

"Okay?" I repeat with a grin of relief.

"Yes. Oh, my god, yes! Why are we still standing here?" she asks excitedly before she slips out of my arms. Sasha strides over to my bike in her sexy strappy heels and white dress. It's way too short for riding on the back of a Harley, which is exactly why I fucking love it. She throws one of her mile-long legs over the seat and then leans forward to grip the handlebars, pushing her amazing ass out and causing her full, perfect tits to nearly spill out of the top of her dress.

"Hop on the back. I'll drive us to the airport," Sasha jokes.

"Goddamn, you are so fucking sexy sitting on my Fat Boy," I tell her. Unable to resist getting a photo of her looking like the pin-up girl from every man's wet dream, I pull out my cell phone from my pocket and snap a picture.

After I put my phone away, I go over and climb on behind her. Smoothing my hands up both of her sides, I whisper to her, "*This* is where you fucking belong. Your fine ass was made to sit on my bike." I bury my nose in her long, blonde hair that's lightly blowing in the coastal winds, unable to get enough of her sweet apple scent before my lips go to her neck right below her ear. It's the one spot on her body that I know from months of experience will make her go limp and instantly wet. Sure enough, Sasha shivers and then leans back against my chest, putty in my hands. Fuck, I don't think I'll ever get enough of her. My cock is so hard that riding will be damn near impossible.

"I want you so much, right here, right now. I can't wait a second longer," I whisper in her ear, fucking desperate for her. "If I lift your dress and lower you down onto my cock, you could ride it just like this, and no one would be able to see me buried deep inside of you."

"*Chase*," Sasha moans my name, making my dick swell even more against the fly of my jeans. "Someone could see us," she says.

"Let them watch. I don't give a fuck, because *this* is all mine," I tell Sasha as I ease my hand underneath the front hem of her dress and cup her pussy through her lacy thong.

I know my girl better than anyone, and the thought of someone catching us is turning her on even more. She's been a good girl for the last seventeen years, so she still likes to pretend she's good when, deep down, she's really fucking naughty.

And despite what her parents think, I wasn't a bad influence on her. Hell, I knew she was a virgin, and I wouldn't do more than kiss her the first few times we went out. Sasha was the one who unzipped my pants in the front seat of her Mustang in the school parking lot and started riding my cock, giving her virginity to me before I fucking knew what hit me.

"Chase, please," Sasha begs when she squirms against my hand that hasn't moved the way she wants yet. As she rocks her hips, her ass bumps right against the bulge in the front of my jeans that's pressing into her bottom and making me fucking crazy.

"You're gonna come on my fingers, and then I'm gonna fuck you right here," I warn her as I slip my fingers underneath the seam of her panties and penetrate her with just the tip of one.

"*Ohhh God*," she moans as she throws her head back on my shoulder, then covers my hand with her own to force me to go deeper inside of her.

My lips come down on her neck again as my fingers start pumping in and out of her already dripping wet pussy. Her walls clamp down on them, and then her entire body shudders as her orgasm slams into her that damn fast for me.

I don't even give her a chance to recover before I remove my hand from her panties and start undoing my jeans as quick as my shaking hands can go, unable to wait another second to be inside of her. And because she's been on birth control for months, there's no rubber needed.

"Hold those handlebars for me, sweetheart," I tell Sasha, who is still panting when she follows my order. Grasping her hip to hold it steady, I fist my cock with the other hand to line up and slam inside of her pussy so hard she cries out.

"Oh, God, Chase!" she moans. Looking at me over her shoulder, Sasha says, "You feel so good."

"Fuck, yes, baby. Ride me just like that," I tell her. She's hot, tight, and wet. So goddamn perfect that I know I won't last long.

My hands grip both of her hips through her dress, tight enough to leave bruises as I slam her down on my cock over and over again.

Reaching up, I gather her hair in a ponytail and give it a harsh tug to turn her face to the side so I can kiss her. "I love you...so fucking much," I tell her against her lips.

"I love you too...*ohhh!*" she shouts as she comes again, forcing me to follow.

As we both catch our breath and come back down from the clouds together, I kiss her neck and down to her shoulder.

Having Sasha in my arms tonight is so goddamn perfect. Knowing she's agreed to be mine forever makes me fucking euphoric, except...for whatever reason, that happiness is accompanied by something else. My guts are knotting up with fear or...or panic. I've never loved anyone this much before, and it's fucking terrifying worrying about screwing everything up with her.

Are we rushing things? I know I'm ready to marry Sasha, but we're both still young. What if I'm pushing her into something that she'll later regret? We both still have a year of high school left, and then she wants to go to college and study journalism. I'd never try to hold her back on purpose; but what if, by marrying her, she gives up on her dreams to be with me instead?

"Are you sure you want to be my old lady?" I ask her into the silence. "You know I won't ever walk away from the MC, and you want to go to college..."

"I want you more," she says as she reaches behind her to run her fingers through my hair. "And who said I couldn't have you and a degree?"

Still unconvinced, I tell her, "It may not always be easy for us. I'll probably piss you off. There's a reason everyone thinks I'm an asshole."

"We'll have good times and bad," she agrees. "But I love every part of you, even the MC and asshole pieces. They're what make you who you are, Chase."

This.

This is why I fucking love this woman so goddamn much. I don't know why the hell I'm even second-guessing her. She's all in right there with me. And unlike some old ladies, she would never ask me to walk away from the club. She knows how important wearing the Savage Kings patch one day soon is to me.

Bringing her face to mine, I kiss the shit out of her until we both have to pull away for oxygen.

"Okay," I say, pushing aside all of those ridiculous doubts or worries, whatever the hell they are. Nothing will change how I feel about Sasha. Ever.

"To the airport?" Sasha asks me when I climb off the back of my bike.

Reaching for her helmet from the handlebar, I kiss the top of her golden head before I put it on her. "Fuck yes," I agree while fastening her chin strap.

Once her helmet is good and secure, I grab mine and get it in place while Sasha scoots backward to her seat, and I take my place in the front.

"You ready, sweetheart?" I ask when I crank the engine.

"Always," Sasha says. Her words and her arms tightening around my waist so close that the front of her body is flush against my back lets me know she's ready to ride with me, not just today but every fucking day for the rest of our lives. She trusts me to take care of her and keep her safe.

I may have been a cold bastard before we met, but she makes me softer because I want to be good to her, good *for* her.

But deep down I've always known that what her parents say about me is true – she deserves better than me, and one of these days I'm probably gonna hurt her beyond repair.

We've stopped for a moment at an intersection, so I reach back to pat her leg reassuringly. Just touching her helps clear the morbid thoughts from my mind.

As the light turns green and the car in front of us clears the intersection, I drop my Fat Boy into gear and ease the throttle, smiling as Sasha reflexively tightens her grip.

The sudden screeching of tires drowns out the roar of my engine. I catch a brief glance of headlights to my right, just before I'm launched into the air.

The next few seconds seem to stretch out endlessly as my body is hurled across the highway. I spin helplessly, briefly blinded by the headlamp on my Harley as my bike's shattered frame twists and sparks across the pavement beneath me. Before I can scream out for Sasha, gravity snatches me back, slamming me into the weedy ditch at the side of the road.

...

A piercing light shines directly into my eyes. When the light disappears, I'm finally able to make out the face, one of a man I've never seen before hovering over me just inches away in the darkness.

"Who...who the fuck ...wh-what the hell...happened?" I gasp. I try to force myself to sit up but fall back as a nauseating wave of vertigo washes over me.

"You had a wreck," the stranger's voice tells me slowly. "Try not to move. We're gonna get you to the hospital."

Wreck? Hospital?

My eyes squint as I try to put the world back into focus to figure out what the fuck's happening. The last thing I remember is sitting in the tattoo chair with Sasha beside me; then we were outside the shop on my bike...

Oh, fuck!

"*Sasha*?" I shout in a panic as I struggle to try and sit up again. The asshole with the light pushes my shoulders back down. To hell with him. I shove him out of the way as I sit up again and see the colorful lights of ambulances, firetrucks, and police cars surrounding us.

Then I spot her; Sasha's body is strapped down on a gurney that's being rushed toward an ambulance.

"*SASHA*!" I scream louder and wait for her to answer me, to tell me that she's okay, but she doesn't make a sound.

CHAPTER ONE

Chase

Present day...

IF THERE'S JUST ONE SINGLE THING THAT EVERY PERSON SHOULD know, it's that you should *never* fuck with a man who has nothing to lose.

Johnny here in the shitty little Ace of Spades MC hasn't learned that lesson just yet, which is why I'm slamming his ugly ass face into the bar counter over and over again until he finally gets the message.

"Sorry...I'm sorry," he mutters as blood pours from his nose and mouth. I'm pretty sure I saw one of his teeth go flying across the room.

"I don't want you to be fucking sorry," I lean down and growl into his ear while I keep his head flattened on the counter. "I want you to stop selling your nasty ass shit in my city. Because if just *one* more person ODs from crank again, I'm gonna come back and see you. And I won't give a damn if you sold it to the fucker or not. It's gonna be your brains blown out on the bar to send a message to anyone else who is dealing. Am I making myself fucking clear?"

"Y-yes," Johnny agrees.

"Good," I say when I finally let his head go. He slumps down to the floor, clutching his newly rearranged face.

Looking up at the bartender, the club's enforcer, who is twice my size but smart enough not to try and interfere with my beat down, I sit down on one of the bar stools and tell him, "We'll take fifteen grand in cash for the funeral expenses and be on our way."

The man simply nods his head and disappears into the back.

"Fuck, man," my best friend Abe mutters as he climbs up on the stool next to me. "Don't ever let me get on your bad side again."

"I'm so fucking sick of this shit," I tell him with a shake of my head as I glance down and see the crimson splatters of blood painting the white t-shirt under my cut. I really should wear red tees more often. "What do you think it's gonna take to keep the roaches out of our town?" I ask Abe.

Lowering his voice to nothing more than a deep rumble, he says, "We're gonna have to start taking these assholes out. Nothing else is working. Three tweakers in the morgue are three too many for one goddamn week."

"No shit," I grumble.

The Savage Kings MC rule the town of Emerald Isle with an iron fist. To most people on the outside, I'm sure our city looks like a biker's paradise. And it is, most of the time. But the MC took on the responsibility of expanding our tourist business; and if you want to keep your house clean for visitors, you have to take out all the trash.

Rival MCs and gangs try to push their hardcore drugs on the tourists to make some easy cash. That shit doesn't fly with us. So, when we find the assholes responsible, we kick them to the curb. That also means the club constantly makes new enemies. So far, we've been able to keep the assholes beat down, but I have no doubt that one of these days our past sins will come back to bite us in the ass.

"Here you go," the bartender says when he finally comes back with a folded up paper bag.

"Took your sweet ass time, didn't you," I remark as he hands over the bag. Opening it up, I look inside and pull out the wad of cash, quickly thumbing through each stack to make sure it's enough.

"Don't make us come back again," I look down and tell the president of their club, who is still sitting on the floor, before I fold up the bag and climb off the barstool.

Abe and I are about to walk out the door when a redhead steps into our path.

"Are you boys leaving already?" she asks in her sultry voice. She hooks her thumbs in the belt loops of her painted-on jeans to make her fake tits stick out even further in her V-neck blouse. "I didn't even get to talk to you yet."

Fuck.

Knowing Abe has a weakness for gingers, I shake my head and answer for both of us before he can.

"We need to get on the road. Maybe next time, honey," I say, trying to blow her off as nice as I can.

The truth is, while fucking new pussy can be great, I prefer to stick to the loyal bitches back in our clubhouse. It makes things a lot easier when the girls know the drill upfront and don't expect anything else from me. They sit, speak, and roll over on command like they've been trained to do. Then, when we're finished, all it takes is one word, and they leave. Nice and simple. They may want more, but I've made it clear that's never gonna fucking happen.

I've only loved one woman enough to want to make her my old lady, and a million random biker sluts will never equal even one of her.

"Aw, come on, Chase," Abe whines as he reluctantly follows me out. "She was hot as fuck and would've done us both at the same time."

"She was Aces' pussy, numb-nuts. She'd gladly distract us long enough with her tits and ass to give them time to shove a knife in our backs. No fucking thank you," I say as I throw a leg over my Street Glide and fasten on my helmet.

"Fine," Abe huffs as he gets on his bike. "I'm hurtin' bad now, so can we at least go straight back to the clubhouse where I *can* fuck something?"

"Hell yes," I tell him with a grin, then start up the engine, ready to get home myself. "Try and keep up," I yell to Abe as his bike thunders to life. Before he can reply, I take off, heading for the highway. There are a few curvy backroads that we have to take to get there, and I like to see how fast I can hang them.

Speeding down an open road on a beautiful summer day with the wind in my face is the only time I ever feel even some hint of peace.

Today my fucking peace doesn't last very long.

I spot the black SUV as soon as it appears in my rearview, about a quarter of a mile behind me and Abe, who has finally caught up. Whoever the fuck's behind the wheel must be in a hurry, because they come roaring up on our asses like a bat out of hell.

When the motherfucker starts to pass us on the curvy, one-lane road, warning flags go off in my head. "Hell no!" I shout as I drop a gear and twist the throttle, gunning it so they can't get in front of me.

Apparently, they didn't actually want to pass us; they just wanted to get our attention when they pull up beside us in the oncoming traffic lane. If their driving didn't get us to notice them, the goddamn barrel of a sawed-off shotgun pointing out the passenger window at us does the fucking trick.

I glance back at Abe, who is on my right, to make sure he saw it too. With a single nod of his head, he slows down, and I do the same, knowing we're sitting ducks on the road, unprotected with a gun pointing right at us.

I ease off onto the gravel shoulder first with Abe behind me. Then, the fucker in the SUV falls back to pull in after him.

By the time I climb off my bike, three men, all wearing goofy ass zoot suits, are already out of their ride, the gun still pointing in our direction.

Taking off my helmet, I hang it on the handlebar and stride toward them.

"What the fuck do you want?" I bark, not giving a shit about my attitude. I'm no longer intimidated by the gun either. If they wanted us dead, they would've pulled the trigger already when they caught us off guard and unarmed. These assholes just want to talk.

"Hands up," the shorter man in the front of the trio with the gun snaps. I roll my eyes, but Abe and I put our palms up in the air, waiting for the men to come closer.

When they do, the dick with the gun gets a little too close to Abe.

"Get your fuckin' gun out of my fuckin' face," Abe growls at the man in warning.

"Or what, big guy. Whatcha gonna do?" the little man asks, thinking he's tough and safe because he's holding a weapon. Guess he can't read or doesn't know the definition of the word *Savage* on the back of our fucking cuts.

My best friend has an even worse temper than me; it just takes longer for it to be unleashed. A gun in his face will definitely unleash it.

When Abe smirks down at the asshole from underneath his thick black beard, I know what he's going to do before the man with the gun does. Dude has always been a savage beast with zero fucks to give.

Abe's elbow comes swinging around and smashes right into the fucker's nose so hard blood pours from it. He screams like a pussy and drops his gun to clench his nose.

"You son of a bitch!" the asshole yells as he and Abe both start to go for the abandoned gun on the ground.

Before either one can pick it up, there's an ear-splitting *POP! POP!* getting everyone's attention. One of the other guys pulled out his gun and fired it right into Abe's bike, blowing out both of the damned tires. The bike jerks forward as the tires collapse; and with a tired creak, the kickstand folds and Abe's baby topples over.

"What the fuck?" Abe bellows as he starts to lurch forward. I throw my arm out in front of his chest to hold him back.

"Everyone needs to calm the fuck down and listen up!" the fucker, who has now assumed the leadership position of the rat pack, tells us as he aims his handgun at us.

"Settle down, Abe," I warn my best friend before he goes off again and makes these guys change their mind about killing us. When he eventually nods, I remove my arm from him.

"Just get on with it already," I say to the assholes. "What do you want?"

The new gunman looks straight at me and says, "We've got a message for your brother." My teeth clench in anger because, for whatever reason, I know he's referring to Torin, my brother by blood and not just one of my MC brothers. "Time's running out, so tell Torin that the boss wants *all* of his money by Friday, or everyone Torin knows is gonna fucking suffer."

If possible, my teeth grind together even harder. I try to reel in my rage before I pound the asshole into the ground for threatening my brother. Hell, he's threatening all of us.

"Got it?" the dickhead asks. "Or should I write all that down for you?"

"Yeah, I've got it," I grit out.

"Good. Glad to hear that," the asshole replies.

The three guys slowly start to back away toward their SUV; the one that's bleeding in a bigger hurry to leave than the other two. As soon as they're inside the vehicle, they hook the wheel hard to do a U-turn, tires kicking up dirt and gravel before they straighten out the SUV and speed away.

"What the fuck was that about? And why the hell did they have to fuck over *my* bike?" Abe grumbles as he walks over and kicks one of the ruined tires.

"You better call Turtle to bring the flatbed," I tell Abe as I stomp over and pick up the sawed-off gun the fuckers left behind. It's a double-barrel, so I crack it open to make sure it's loaded. It is.

"Turtle?" Abe asks. "Fuck, you know he'll take his sweet ass time."

"Then tell him to get his ass in gear!" I reply, shoving the gun into the saddle bag that only covers about half of it and straddling my bike while quickly putting my helmet back on.

"Where the hell are you going?" Abe asks.

"No one gets away with threatening the fucking Kings, especially not those idiots," I explain.

"You're going after them?" Abe asks before he jogs over to my bike. "Shit, at least let me ride with you. I can shoot while you drive."

"Sorry, man, but you know I never let anyone fucking ride with me," I remind him. No one, not a single club slut, has been on the back of my bike in ten years. "Just get out of here as fast as you can, yeah?"

Abe curses. "This isn't smart, Chase."

"Since when am I ever smart?" I ask with a grin before I start my bike. I make a U-turn in the middle of the road, then take off after the SUV. Since there's only the shitty ass Aces bar in this small coastal town, there's just one place they could be headed – the highway.

It doesn't take me long to catch up to them since a Harley is a helluva lot faster than an SUV. They abide by the speed limit; I don't. There are no traffic rules that I follow while weaving in and out of traffic to get closer.

I stay behind a box truck so they can't see me until traffic clears up ahead. Then, I pull out the sawed-off from my bag and gun the engine up the left lane.

Holding the throttle with my right hand, I angle the shotgun over my handlebar and shoot with the left.

BOOM!

I unload into the rear tire and then race up beside them to fire the second barrel into the driver's window before they know what hit them. The SUV swerves off the right side of road, probably because the man driving is dead or badly hurt. They were going more than sixty miles an hour, so in my rearview, I watch them flip at least two times before I disappear down the highway.

Now, I just need to figure out who the hell they were and why they were threatening my brother.

CHAPTER TWO

Sasha Sheridan

THE SCATTERED WRECKAGE FROM THE AUTO ACCIDENT ALONG the highway brings back a lot of shitty memories. Ones that I've tried to forget over the past ten years, without any luck. And no, it wasn't the pain of the four surgeries or even the agonizing year of physical therapy that was the hardest to overcome. The worst part was going through it all without the man who said he loved me and wanted to marry me.

When I woke up in the hospital after my first surgery, Chase wasn't there.

And I was so fucking angry at him for bailing on me that I refused to call him to ask why.

After the first few days, reading the articles in the paper, I started to think Chase disappeared from my life because he felt guilty, that he may blame himself for not being able to get out of the way of the drunk driver who hit us.

If that was the case, though, then why didn't he just come and tell me that? I would've assured him that it wasn't his fault and that he didn't do anything wrong, except run away when I needed him the most.

But my pride wouldn't give in and seek him out first. Weeks went by, and then months while I kept waiting for him to come around. I missed my entire senior year of high school, including prom and graduation. While my friends were partying, I was struggling through therapy and homeschooling. My choices for college were narrowed down significantly after the year out of school and without having any extracurricular activities to pad my applications, so I ended up going right down the road to the University of North Carolina at Wilmington. I was at least able to convince my parents to let me stay in the dorms like a normal college student. But I haven't felt normal for one day in the ten years since the accident.

When I graduated with my journalism degree, I landed a job working at the local television station. My dream had always been to travel the world as an international correspondent, reporting from the most exciting places on Earth. For some stupid reason, I haven't been able to make myself leave the state where *he* still lives. After ten years, I think a part of me has still been waiting for Chase Fury to find me and give me an explanation for why he broke my heart.

Most of the people who see me on television will never even know about the ordeal I've been through. That's because fixing up my busted face was a pretty easy procedure for the plastic surgeons. My new chin and nose turned out better than before the accident, but even after all this time, my face still looks a little foreign to me when I catch a glimpse of myself in a mirror. The hardest part was trying to repair my knee. I never wear dresses or any clothing on the air that reveals the thick, four-inch scar that runs over my kneecap. The damn thing is so fucked up that, after several surgeries to put in pins and screws, I still walk with a slight limp. It always hurts whenever rain is on the way, making me wonder if I should've been a meteorologist instead of a reporter.

I shouldn't be complaining, because I know that the weeks of recovering in the hospital and months in physical therapy required for me to walk again were nothing compared to what could've happened to me. The doctors said I was lucky to be alive, unlike one of the victims of the wreck we're here reporting on today. At the time, I didn't feel very lucky because I lost something that could never be replaced.

"Sasha, are you ready?" Steve, our cameraman, asks me. "Sergeant Barnes, you good to go?"

"Yes," the deep voice of the uniformed man I had forgotten was next to me answers.

Nodding my agreement as well, I push aside the memories of my past, straighten my red WBRL polo shirt with my free hand and grip the microphone in the other. Then, I wait until Steve holds up his three fingers and counts down. When he gets to one, I launch into my rehearsed spiel.

"I'm here on the scene of a serious accident involving at least one fatality on highway seventeen south in New Hanover County. Authorities are still investigating the cause of the wreck. With me this afternoon is Sergeant Barnes of the Highway Patrol. Sergeant Barnes, what can you tell us about this horrible accident?" I ask as I tilt the microphone toward the tall man's face.

"Well, based on the bullet holes on the vehicle's driver's side, we believe that this could have been an unfortunate road rage incident turned tragic. We do have a witness who says she saw a single white male ride up on a black Harley-Davidson motorcycle and fire a gun into the victim's SUV. If anyone has any additional information about the possible gunman, please call our local office. The suspect is believed to have been wearing motorcycle gang insignia on a leather vest or jacket."

A chill goes up my spine. I can't help but think about the leather-wearing man from my past who still haunts my present.

"Do you have any suspects?" I ask the sergeant.

"Not yet, but there are only a few motorcycle clubs in the area who are known to wear the bearded skull patch that our witness was able to draw for us, pointing our investigation in a very clear direction."

"Oh shit," I mutter, knowing that exact bearded skull logo all too well. The Savage Kings are *killers* now? Is that the type of man Chase turned into? I guess anything is possible after ten years. I'm starting to think I never really knew him...

"Cut!" Steve says before he lowers the heavy camera from his shoulder. "Sasha, once again, watch the language!"

"Sorry," I apologize with a cringe.

"Let's wrap this up so we can edit it for the six o'clock news. Jim will be pissed if he has to hold off until the eleven o'clock."

"Okay, I'm ready," I say. Steve gives the signal, and then I pick up where we left off. "Again, if anyone has information that could lead authorities to the suspect responsible, please call the Highway Patrol Office at the number on the bottom of the screen." Steve nods, knowing they'll be happy to plug that number into the clip during editing.

"This has been Sasha Sheridan reporting from New Hanover County for WBRL Seventeen News."

"And cut!" Steve says. "We're good."

Turning to the sergeant, I put the microphone in my left hand to hold out my right for him to shake. "Thank you so much for your help."

"Anytime. It was a pleasure," he replies with a grin as he clutches my hand in his strong grip. "I mean, I feel awful about the victims, but I'm glad I got to meet you."

"Oh, um, right," I agree.

"Besides," he says as he steps closer and lowers his voice, "Off the record, these guys have criminal records a mile long. They were all wanted."

Why does hearing that make me feel better? It shouldn't. Three men are still badly injured and at least one is dead because of one of the Savage Kings.

"Did the witness describe the biker?" I ask.

"Well, she said he had light hair and a pretty thick beard, both almost a reddish-blond color. She wasn't absolutely sure, so we won't be sharing that with the public. She also noticed several tattoos covering his right arm, but keep that between us too, okay? We need to hold a few of our cards to verify any witness information that comes forward."

"Okay," I agree, even though speaking that one word is difficult. While I haven't seen Chase Fury in years, the description may very well be a match for him. All except for the beard, which he could've grown out. Would he do something so...so brutal?

Removing his hat and running his fingers through his short, dark hair, the sergeant says, "So, um, would you maybe want to have dinner with me sometime?"

"Ah, well, um." Caught off guard, I stammer, which is unusual since I thought my public speaking courses beat all of those sentence fillers out of me. I'm still working on the potty mouth.

"Here, how about I give you my card; and if you come to a decision, you just let me know?" Sergeant Barnes suggests. Pulling out his wallet, he reaches inside and pulls out his business card, complete with the shiny badge logo and all.

"Wow, okay," I say when I take the card. He's a nice looking guy, tall and muscular like I prefer. Besides, I haven't had a date in...okay, longer than I care to admit.

"Have a good one," Sergeant Barnes says. He puts his big hat back on and tugs down the front brim at me like a cowboy.

As I watch him walk away, I notice his nice plump ass in his uniform; but other than that, there's no real spark. Which is a shame. He's just too...nice. I need...well, I need a little bit of a bad boy to keep things interesting.

Blowing out a breath, I make my way back to our news van and climb inside for a drink of water to try and wrap my head around the breaking news.

Before, I stayed away from Chase because I refused to be the one to break the silence when he's the one who hurt me. I don't mean physically, like I'm sure he thinks, but the emotional damage that he caused. Now, though, my curiosity has been raised about the Savage Kings. Since they have charters all over the United States, if I broke a story about them going around killing people on the highway in broad daylight, it could have the potential to go national.

Besides, even if I don't write one word of a story, I still need to know the kind of man Chase has become. There was a brief moment in time when I was planning to spend the rest of my life with him. Maybe, if I find out that he's turned into a killer, I'll finally be able to let him go once and for all.

CHAPTER THREE

Chase

I PULL UP BACK AT THE CLUBHOUSE A FEW MINUTES BEFORE Abe and Turtle roll up in the flatbed with Abe's bike strapped on the back, giving me enough time to stash the cash from the Aces in our vault to distribute to the families of our OD victims before I head back outside.

"Guess you survived after all," Abe says when he climbs out of the cab. "Did you find them?

"Can we go talk somewhere else?" I ask him quietly.

"Yeah, sure," he replies.

"Let's take a walk to the pier," I suggest, since there's one near the clubhouse. It's the only place that you can always trust that your conversation will be confidential. It's easy to make sure nobody else is around, and the waves drown out the sound for any recording devices.

On the way, I pull out a smoke and light it up, taking a long draw before blowing it out to try and calm my nerves.

Once we get to the end of the pier, Abe and I turn around to face the busy boardwalk, putting our backs to the rail to keep an eye out for anyone approaching.

"So, did you fucking hit them?" he asks.

"Yeah. The SUV flipped a few times. Don't know if they survived; those boys didn't seem bright enough to figure out seatbelts. I'm sure we'll find out later.," I tell him. "Did you say anything to Turtle?" I ask.

"Nah. He knows better than to ask questions. He just laughed when he saw the flat tires. Probably thinks you did it being a dick."

"If anyone asks, I did it," I agree. Taking another drag from my smoke, I blow it out and grin. "Since I am a dick, it shouldn't be a hard sell."

"No shit," Abe agrees with a chuckle. Crossing his arms over his chest, he looks over at me and arches a dark eyebrow. "So, why don't you want Turtle or anyone else to know what went down with those assholes?"

"You heard those guys. Torin is in some sort of deep shit. He owes someone. I don't know who, but I want a few days to try and get answers from him before we blow the whole thing up with the entire club."

"Okay, that makes sense," Abe agrees. I know I can trust him to keep his mouth shut. The two of us have had each other's backs since the first day we met in prison. Well, after I socked the big man in the jaw.

"Torin's gonna be pissed when he finds out you went after those fuckers without checking with him first," he says.

As the president of the MC, Torin pulls weight over me, his VP.

"I had to make a split-second decision. It wasn't like I could call him to ask permission and still have time to catch up to them," I grumble.

"And you know that if you *had* called him, he would've told you to stand the fuck down."

That's where my brother and I differ. He spent a few years in the Army while I was here holding shit together for the MC. I patched in way before him, when I was just nineteen. But when our uncle died, Torin had been back a few years and was already handling most of the MC's businesses dealings. He wanted the gavel and was voted in, which was fine by me. I wasn't cut out for leadership, because I don't play well with others.

The thing is, though, during those years apart, Torin developed one set of morals in the Army, and I have an entirely different set...if I even have any at all. Half the MC table is former military who couldn't find a fit in civilian life when they returned from the desert. The other half of our members are mostly criminals and convicts like me who served time and don't know how to do anything but the outlaw shit. Torin knows that sometimes you have to cross a few lines to get business handled and dole out justice. If you wait for the rest of the world to do it, you'll die before it ever gets served. That's why sometimes you have to take matters into your own fucking hands to balance the scales. And I don't regret handing out my own brand of retribution that landed me in the Big House for fourteen months. It was worth it, and I deserved it.

"Let me know if you need anything from me, yeah?" Abe asks as he pushes off the rail.

"You fucking know it," I tell him. Taking one last pull on my smoke, I put it out in one of the ashtray buckets bolted down onto the wood. We may be a bunch of savages, but we don't fuck up our beaches.

"Shit, what time is it?" I ask aloud, having gotten distracted by all of today's excitement and the long drive back to town. Obviously I took some detours just to make sure no one else tailed me.

"Probably around five-thirty or so," Abe says as we both pull out our phones to check.

"Damn, I gotta get back to the clubhouse," I say when I realize it's already a quarter to six. "I'll go talk to Torin later."

"What the hell is it that you do every afternoon in your room? You take a nap or some shit?" Abe teases as we start walking back.

"Fuck you," I tell him as I flip him the finger with a grin. "It's none of your fucking business."

"Well, I don't know about you, but I plan to spend the rest of my evening with a beautiful redhead."

"Which one?" I ask. "Becky or Cynthia?"

"Either. Both. You know I don't give a shit," Abe replies with a smirk. "You can keep your blondes. Reds are way more fucking fun."

"If you say so," I tell him with a shake of my head.

He's right, though. I rarely take women back to my room unless my cock is hurting so bad that I'm forced to find it a warm, wet place to get some relief before it explodes. And when that happens, they're always blonde. It's been two weeks since I had something besides my hand to keep me company, so maybe I'll look for someone when we get back to the clubhouse. God knows there's always an endless supply of easy riders lurking in the *Savage Asylum,* the bar above where our chapter holds church, and about six of us have basic apartments with a bed and bathroom. Some of the guys have houses, like Torin and War, but they also have families. My single brothers and I prefer to stay where the action is easily accessible for whenever we need a warm body. For a few of my more rowdy brothers, that's all night, every fucking night.

After you've had the classiest, sexiest, most gorgeous woman ever to walk the earth, it's hard to get real excited about biker sluts who'll fuck any bastard in a leather cut. Those girls shouldn't want me or my brothers to put them on their knees, but we can't seem to get rid of them. In fact, a few more show up every week, ready and willing to let us use their bodies however we see fit. They know that they may not get anything in return, or they may get fucked rough and dirty, but that's the best they can hope for. We make no other promises.

Which is why I only feel a little guilty when I walk into the bar and crook my finger at Nikki, one of our loyals who's been coming around the club for several months now. I've used her mouth a few times before and know she's a goddamn champ at deep throating.

She never whines, bitches, or gives me a fake fucking pout when I kick her out either. And the best part about Nikki? She's a natural blonde, just like I like, not that mustard yellow fake shit that's too god awful for me to even pretend they're someone else.

As soon as she's following me, I go over and punch in the code to get in the basement before she can see it. We change the code every week, and only members and their guests are allowed downstairs.

I keep my apartment door locked to prevent my brothers from stealing all my smokes and condoms, so I pull out the key to turn the lock. I push the door open for Nikki, who thank fuck, still hasn't said a word, to walk through first.

Locking the door behind us, I grab the remote to turn on the flat screen sitting on top of the dresser which brings up channel seventeen; then I put it on mute.

"You know what to do," I tell Nikki when I take a seat at the foot of the bed in front of the flat screen. Without needing further instructions, she kneels down in her tight, sleeveless black dress between my legs and undoes my jeans while I lay back on my elbows.

My cock hasn't even started getting hard yet when it bobs free from my jeans.

Wrapping her hand around my shaft, all it takes is a few teasing flicks of her tongue over the tip to cause the blood to finally rush down and make it lengthen, because I'm a grower *and* a goddamn shower.

Before I can even warn her to stop teasing me and get to work sucking, Nikki opens her mouth and takes every inch of me into her throat.

"Fuck, yes. Just like that," I tell her as I cup the back of her bobbing head to speed her up. She sucks my cock so good for so long that her jaw has to be hurting, but Nikki doesn't stop or complain.

I'm nowhere close to being able to come, not until *her* face appears on the television screen behind Nikki.

"Oh, fuck," I groan, because I swear Sasha gets a little more stunning each day. She's standing outside, so the wind gently picks up her long blonde hair, making it dance around her face.

I let out a growl when the camera zooms out and shows some asshole standing beside her, way too close. He's a fucking cop on top of that.

Fingernails reach for my stomach, almost distracting me from the screen as they move up my abs and try to push up my shirt.

"No," I say, and Nikki backs off of it right away.

I don't take my shirt off around anyone. I can't bear to hear them say her name aloud or ask me who she is when they see my ink.

Watching Sasha again, my eyes zero in on her right hand holding the microphone, but like usual, there's not even a trace of my name on her wrist anymore. She erased every part of me from her life and it fucking kills me.

When Nikki's moans vibrate around my cock, I realize that I'm probably pulling her hair a little too hard.

"Play with my balls and suck me faster," I tell her since I'm losing my hard-on.

Looking back up at the screen, the news camera pans over behind Sasha to the wreckage that makes me cringe as it brings up the horrid memories of that night I was with her. When I was finally able to get the doctors to release me at hospital so I could see Sasha, she was still unconscious, getting prepped for surgery. Her face was covered in blood, and her knee was a nightmare, twisted in ways it should never go. The woman I loved was lying there in complete disarray, and it was all my fault.

When the screen zooms in on bullet holes in the side of a black SUV that's totaled and half burnt, I get to my feet so fast, Nikki almost falls backward before she catches herself.

Reaching behind me for the remote on the mattress, I unmute it and rewind to hear the whole story.

And son of a fucking bitch.

It's the wreck I caused, and now I know without a doubt that I killed at least one of those men and messed up the other two. So does everyone else up and down the coast.

Fuck.

"What's wrong, baby?" Nikki asks.

"Get out," I growl, without even sparing her a glance.

"But I didn't finish you off yet. I can do better, I swear."

"Later," I tell her as I tuck my dick into my jeans and zip back up.

Finally, Nikki gets the hint and leaves without another word. I should've walked her back upstairs, but I can't stop rewinding the news clip. One thing stands out each time – they know it was a member of the Savage Kings, but hopefully, they don't know it was me.

We're gonna need to get a lawyer who can hopefully find a way to keep my ass out of prison.

And whoever those guys were working for, I'm sure they've already reported that Torin's brother didn't want to hear their shit. Depending on who these guys are, the club and I could be in for some serious retribution.

I guess it's time I finally have that talk with Torin.

CHAPTER FOUR

Chase

"JESUS FUCK, PEOPLE!" I GRUMBLE AS I SLAP MY PALM OVER MY eyes to shield them from the atrocities I just witnessed.

"Sorry, Chase," Kennedy, Torin's wife, giggles from underneath him, not the least bit ashamed that I walked up on Torin bending her over the MC's table.

"You ever think of closing the damn door?" I ask while fumbling around behind me to find the doorknob and pull it shut while I wait for them to finish.

I get it — not many of us hang around downstairs until later on in the night, but fuck. I do not need to see my brother with his dick out.

Instead of listening to them outside the door, I go back to wait in my room. Of course, I sit down on the bed and continue watching the WBRL News, telling myself I want to see if there's any additional information about the accident and that I'm not just hoping to see her face again.

Eventually, Kennedy sticks her head in my open door. "He's all yours now," she tells me with a grin, her cheeks still flushed from the fucking.

"I thought you had better manners, Kennedy," I tease my sister-in-law when I get to my feet.

"Usually I do," she replies as she rests her hands on her baby bump that's now big enough to have its own area code, not that I would tell her that. "But I'm trying to get this baby out, which means getting it in whenever I can. The doctor says sex will sometimes put you into labor."

"Any day now, right?" I ask with a grin, excited to meet my nephew.

"Any fucking day," she replies with a heavy exhale. "I'm headed home. Try and get Torin out of here before midnight, if you can."

"I'll try," I tell her before she leaves.

My brother doesn't fuck around with any of the girls upstairs. He'd never cheat on Kennedy, because he knows how much it would hurt her, especially while she's waddling around with his enormous spawn trying to kick its way out. But Torin does stay late most nights, dealing with the headache that comes with running about six different legit businesses as well as being the original charter for a growing MC.

Turning off my television, I stroll back out into the hallway and down to the chapel, the room where we hold our MC meetings. Like usual, Torin is back to work, sitting at the head of the table, reading through the stack of papers in front of him that a naked Kennedy recently occupied. I know it can't be easy for him to oversee all of the MC's legit shit and deal with our grow operation and distribution, but Torin never bitches. He's a better man than me.

"Hey, what's up?" he asks when he sees me come in. Leaning back in his chair with his hands behind his head and a goofy grin on his face, he's the epitome of a man who just got laid. I hate to say I'm jealous of him and what he has with Kennedy. Mostly because I had that once and I fucked it up.

It sucks, but now I'm gonna have to burst my brother's happy little bubble.

Shutting the door behind me to make sure we're not interrupted or overheard, I tell him, "I need to talk to you."

"Okay?" he says as he lowers his arms and rests them on the table in front of him to get serious. I take my usual seat on his right.

"Abe and I got pulled over today," I start. "Not by blue lights, but by a gun barrel."

"What the fuck?" he exclaims.

I fill Torin in on the rest, the exact words the men told me to tell him about the Friday deadline, along with my pursuit that left at least one of the fuckers dead.

"Goddammit, Chase!" Torin roars as he pushes his chair away from the table and gets up to pace. Both of his hands threaten to pull all of his short, dirty blond hair out. "What were you even doing at the Aces' bar?"

"Goddamn me?" I reply definsively as I lean back in my chair. "You know why I paid a visit to the Aces – they've been branching out and slinging some hard drugs. We've had at least three ODs in town that we know they're behind. I warned them to stop and made them cough up money for the funerals. There's fifteen grand in the safe to pay for them. You're fucking welcome. Now, how about you back the fuck up and tell me what the hell is going on with you? Who do you owe money to, Torin?"

"None of your fucking business," he snaps, just like I did at Abe earlier when he wanted to know what I do every night at six o'clock. My shit with Sasha is personal, so whatever is going on with Torin must hit close to home with his old lady.

"None of my business? Really?" I reply. "I think it suddenly became my business when Abe and I got pulled over at gunpoint by some rat pack assholes."

"Just stay out of it," Torin says while his size fourteen boots continue to burn holes in the carpet with his pacing. "And don't give the Aces any more shit unless I tell you to."

"Someone saw me on the highway gunning the fuckers down! It was on the news. How can I stay out of it now?"

"Any attorney worth their shit can get you out of some vague ass witness description. Besides, we don't own the market on leather cuts with bearded skull patches. Any Kings wannabe could make their own. The cops don't have shit."

"Well, we need to get an attorney locked down in case it comes back on me. And we need to call the Wilmington charter and warn them. I probably should've already given them a heads-up. They're the closest to the scene of the accident, so the cops will hit them up first."

"Do it. Now," Torin orders. I take care of it, getting the charter's VP on the line and summarizing shit for him. Thank fuck Charlie says they haven't had any LEOs busting down their doors yet in Wilmington, which makes me think Torin is right – they don't have enough probable cause to get an arrest warrant for anyone. *Yet.*

"Are we gonna bring this to the table?" I ask Torin when I end the phone call, wanting to know if he's gonna try and keep this shit from his brothers.

"Not tonight," he says.

"Tomorrow?" I ask, because I don't like keeping secrets from our boys, especially if there could be heat coming down on the whole MC with the police investigating. Our stepsister Jade just moved back to town and took over the sheriff's department, so she can keep our asses out of trouble here in Carteret County, but that doesn't mean every other cop in the surrounding counties won't be watching us like hawks.

"Tomorrow," Torin reluctantly agrees. "I'll talk to Jade and ask her to see what she can find out."

"Good," I agree as I get to my feet. Realizing Torin still hasn't told me what the hell he's gotten himself into, I ask, "Are you sure you're okay?"

"Yeah, yeah, it's fine. Don't worry, and don't you dare get

Kennedy riled up about this fucking mess. She doesn't need any stress on her right now with the baby coming any day."

"Yeah, got it," I agree, even though now I'm certain my brother is into some bad shit. He talks to Kennedy about every fucking thing, so the fact that he doesn't want me to say anything to her means he's intentionally keeping her in the dark.

That's a really bad fucking sign.

CHAPTER FIVE

Sasha

"Hi, this is Sasha Sheridan calling from WBRL News with a few quick questions for the sheriff," I say into my cell phone while I wait in a plastic chair at the terminal for my flight.

"Just a moment," the woman replies before putting me on hold.

Finally, after all this time, I'm going to D.C. to interview for an international correspondent position. I'm running out of time and not getting any younger, so it's now or never on applying to a job that lets me travel the world instead of keeping me in the small coastal county that's boring ten out of twelve months a year. The most exciting two months are right now during the summer when there are enough tourists around to spark headlines with shark attacks and other horrible water accidents.

"Jade speaking," a woman's authoritative voice comes over the line.

"Hi, Jade. I'm Sasha Sher– "

"You're a reporter. I know. What's up?" she asks, making me smile when she cuts to the chase. Speaking of, I know she's Chase's stepsister and she probably doesn't remember me, but we all went to high school together. I think she was one year younger than us.

"I just had a few questions for you. Off the record," I reply.

"Shoot."

"Are you aware that the Savage Kings are dealing meth?" I come right out and ask. After staying up late last night researching the names of the three victims of the fatal wreck, I saw one fairly common denominator – methamphetamine convictions. Throw that in with the fact that there have been three overdoses on the stuff in the last week up in Carteret County where the original Savage Kings charter is located, and well, it doesn't take a genius to figure out the Kings could be involved in the drug business. Again, I don't want to believe that's true, but I need to know. Their stepsister, the sheriff, seemed like a good place to start.

"Wow," Jade says after a fairly long pause. "You don't pull any punches, do you, Sasha? Were you this feisty when you were dating my stepbrother?"

Now it's my turn to go speechless. "You, ah, remember that?" I ask.

"You were Chase's high school sweetheart. How could I forget? Especially when he has your name plastered across his chest."

"He still has that tattoo?" I ask before I can stop myself. "Does he have a beard now too?"

"Yes, as far as I know, and yes, unless he shaved it off in the last few days," Jade tells me, making my chest tighten knowing it was him. It had to be. "So are you calling to check up on Chase or what?"

"I think he was the shooter involved in the wreck on highway seventeen yesterday," I tell her in a rush, my voice shaking as I say the words aloud for the first time. "The witness gave a description matching him and saw the MC's logo."

"Holy shit," Jade mutters. Then, "The witness could've been mistaken. The Savage Kings have a rather distinguishing patch. Maybe she's just seen it before and thought that's what she saw yesterday. Eye-witnesses are notoriously wrong about what they think they see after the fact."

"I know, that does happen. But the three victims, Keith Washington, Derek Sutton, and Malcolm Butner are all known meth dealers. Do you think it's a coincidence that they're attacked the same week as three overdoses killed people in Emerald Isle?"

"I-I didn't know that," Jade says, sounding surprised.

"Look, I'm not trying to make the Kings out to be something they're not. Believe me, I would prefer to live in my naïve little world and not know if the man I used to love is now a drug dealer and murderer, but I also need answers about this."

"For a story, or for yourself?" Jade asks.

"Both."

"Look, you know I'm not aware of what my stepbrothers do in the MC, and I never will be. But I really don't think they're bad guys. Torin is incredibly strict with the members. He keeps them in line –"

"Torin met with Hector Cruz this morning," I blurt out, saving the best newsflash for last. "So maybe you don't want to see what's going on, but why else would the president of the MC be meeting with a known meth kingpin unless they were in business together?" I ask.

"There's no way..." Jade starts. "Torin was probably telling him to stay away..."

"I have photos of them having a very casual talk together. If you give me your cell number, I'll send you copies."

Jade's silent a second before she calls out the seven digits. I scramble to find my pen and tiny notepad from my purse so I can jot them down before I forget.

"Got it. I'll send the photos over soon."

"Thanks," Jade replies. "And you know I'm gonna have to go to Torin and Chase about this, right?"

"Yeah. I hope you do and that you're able to get explanations that are better than the ones I'm putting together," I tell her honestly even if I'm a little nervous about her talking to Chase about me. "I'm on my way out of town, but I'll be back tomorrow afternoon if you find out anything."

"Okay. I can't make any promises that I'll be able to share with you, though."

"Understood," I say. "Thanks, Jade."

Ending the call, I pull up my camera roll and then forward the photos I took outside of Hector's pool hall. Once I compiled the three victim's records and realized they were into the meth game, Hector's was my first stop on the way to the airport this morning. Honestly, I didn't expect to even see him there, much less Chase's brother Torin, because the place was closed. But as soon as I spotted them together in the parking lot, I knew I was on to something big.

The locals up and down the coast love the Savage Kings for all that they've done turning the economy around for Carteret County and bringing more tourists through the state. They've provided a ton of jobs with their new businesses. The other charters are known to keep the violence and drugs out of their towns too. The public deserves to know if their beloved Kings are actually poisoning the area with drugs.

And I plan to find out exactly what they're up to. If that means getting closer to the man who broke my heart into a million pieces, so be it.

CHAPTER SIX

Chase

I'M STILL YAWNING THE NEXT MORNING WHEN I'M STANDING outside the chapel, holding the bucket to collect my brothers' phones as they enter our meeting. Torin's already in there; and from the looks of him, I'm not certain he didn't sleep on the table last night.

Sax, our MC's secretary, wanders in first, his perpetual half-grin lighting up his face. He's the only man I've ever seen with a resting laugh face, and I've never known him to be in a bad mood. Hell, he even got his jaw broken once in a fight down in Wilmington, and the son-of-a-bitch was at the bar the next day drinking beer through a straw, smiling ear to ear with his jaw wired shut.

I see Abe towering behind Sax, and give him a nod to thank him for keeping quiet as he drops his flip phone in the bucket. He winks back, then instinctively ducks his head to go through the door to the chapel. The arched doorway is high enough to accommodate the giant brute, but I guess years of bashing his skull on 'normal' doors took a toll on him.

Dalton, our money man, comes in next, stopping just long

enough to show me a picture of his latest conquest on his phone. The pretty little blond bastard pulls in more tail than the rest of the club combined, and I just snort and wave him on as he starts to go through his camera roll for the last few days. I check Cooper in after him, and then have to wait while our tech guy, Reece, digs through his pockets, dropping two phones and what looks like a game console into the bucket.

Fast Eddie limps down the stairs next, holding up the boys behind him. His old ass is slower than Turtle in the mornings, and he's struggling to catch what's left of his brown hair and pull it back into a ponytail when he hustles past me.

Miles, our enforcer while Ian is locked up, is right behind Eddie, and I stop him just long enough to rub his bald dome. "For good luck," I tease him, knowing how much it irritates him. He just shakes his head and makes room for Gabriel, Abe's younger brother, who is thankfully a bit smaller than his sibling.

Gabe pauses by me for a moment, casting a critical eye at the vine of black and white roses tattooed on my upper arm. "You need to get over to the shop and let me touch that up for you, man. You've been getting too much sun, so those lighter areas are fading badly."

"Later," I tell him shortly, waving him on into the room. Gabe runs our tattoo parlor and is always super critical of any ink he didn't do personally. It's not my fault he was still a teenager when I got my sleeve done.

I step back to make room as War brings up the rear of the line. If Abe is almost too tall for the clubhouse, then War is too damned wide. I swear the boy is broader than he is tall, and he's not a short man. I can't even see a phone in his thick hand when he drops it into the bucket; and when he pats my back to usher me into the room, my feet almost leave the ground.

"Listen up!" Torin says, slamming his gavel down from the head of the table to get the guys to shut up and pay attention. I've barely gotten the doors closed, but I'm all ears. I want to know what the fuck's going on with my brother; and now that we're all gathered, we're going to sort this out.

"Some of you may have heard about the wreck on highway seventeen that happened yesterday."

"Yeah."

"Yep."

"Uh-huh."

Most of the guys agree or nod their heads in agreement.

"Well, it seems that our VP went a little cowboy on some meth dealers."

The guys slap their hands on the table in approval while I can't help but think to myself, *How the hell does Torin know that they were meth dealers?*

"Our stepsister Jade got a call from a reporter this morning," Torin says, making my heart start beating triple time.

"Sasha called Jade?" I ask aloud, and the room goes silent.

Torin's eyes narrow in my direction. "Yeah, Sasha Sheridan. How the fuck do you know the reporter?" Before I can respond, his eyes lower to my left pec that remains covered as usual, and he answers his own question since he's seen it before. "Oh. So that's the same Sasha as...?"

"Yeah," I mutter. "One and the same." Since Torin was off in the Army when Sasha and I were together, he doesn't know all the details, just the overview — we dated, I wrecked my bike, she got hurt, and it ended.

"Sasha? The sexy blonde reporter from channel seventeen?" Dalton pipes up and asks from the other end of the table.

"That one," Torin agrees.

"Damn, Chase," Dalton drawls. "You hittin' that fine ass bombshell?"

My glare makes the pretty boy prick cower. "Right. Sorry I asked," he mutters.

"*Anyway,*" Torin says. "There's a witness who saw Chase's cut since he wasn't smart enough to take it off *before* committing capital offenses in broad fucking daylight."

"The assholes threatened Torin and the rest of us," I say in my defense, so they don't think I was just being a hothead going off half-cocked like usual. "I had to follow them and didn't have time to ditch the cut."

"Who the hell were these assholes?" War, Torin's Sergeant in Arms, asks, because it's his responsibility to stand between Torin and any fuckers who try to kill him.

"Hector Cruz's guys," Torin responds, and again I'm wondering how the fuck he knows all this. "Jade and the reporter have put a few things together," he explains. Then, eyeing me, he says, "History or not, we can't have this reporter...chick broadcasting our shit all over the state and bringing more heat on us."

My teeth grind together because I'm pretty sure he was gonna call her the *reporter bitch* but caught himself at the last minute.

"The cops haven't even been to question our Wilmington charter, which means they don't have shit. We can't have her doing their job for them," my brother adds.

"Yeah."

"Agreed."

"Absolutely," the guys around the table agree.

"She won't be a problem," I assure them, but the truth is I haven't spoken to Sasha in ten years, not since I fucked her on my bike before we were supposed to elope. Even if I get on my knees and beg her to keep her nose out of this mess, she doesn't have any reason to do me, the man who abandoned her, any fucking favors.

Still, I can at least warn her that she's on Torin's radar and that I can't protect her if she keeps sticking her nose where it doesn't belong. She should know damn well that I can't protect her from shit, or she wouldn't have ever been laid up in that hospital for weeks, going through God only knows what kind of pain because of me.

I wanted to be there for her. Hell, I *tried* to be there for her, spending days in the waiting room to see her, but her father made it clear that Sasha said she never wanted to see me again, and that she blamed me for every second of pain she was going through.

This time I won't let her down. I'll make sure that she stays clear of this shitstorm that Torin's gotten himself into. Which means, whether she likes it or not, it's time for me to finally pay her a visit.

CHAPTER SEVEN

Sasha

"Hi, Daddy!" I say to my father when he answers the phone.

"Hi, sweetie. How did your interview go this morning?"

"Better than I could've hoped!" I tell him as I walk to my car in the airport parking lot. "The panel I met said that they need to talk to my producer at WBRL and then I would probably be hearing from them in a few days, with an offer!"

"That's great, Sash. I'm happy for you. Finally getting your big break," my father says. "We should celebrate."

"Yeah, and we will soon," I promise him. "But I'm sort of beat from all the traveling yesterday and today, so maybe this weekend?"

"Sure, sweetie. We'll see you then. Love you," he says.

"Love you, too," I reply before ending the call.

While I'm excited about the new opportunity, I'm also a little nervous about making the move to the national news.

God knows I'm self-conscious. Of course, everyone in the public eye is somewhat, but because of my scarring and the changes in my face that aren't my own, I'm super sensitive to the comments assholes sitting behind their computers at home make on social media.

I wish I could avoid those sites altogether, but it's part of the job, socializing and drawing the public in so that they turn on their televisions to WBRL every night.

Still, the whole time I was away, and even when I was in the interview, my mind was wandering. I couldn't stop thinking about the story I uncovered right before I left town. And I was curious to see what Jade came up with and if she would tell me if she had something on the Savage Kings, or if she would protect her stepbrothers. So far, her only response was to acknowledge that it was Torin in the photos.

Tomorrow I'll worry about the drug kingpins and the MC. Tonight is too perfect and beautiful not to climb in my car and enjoy riding home with the top down in my convertible, the warm coastal breeze blowing through my hair.

While the classic convertible that my dad and I rebuilt together isn't as thrilling a ride as being on the back of a Harley, it's as close as I can get since I can't exactly see myself ever getting my motorcycle license. And even after the accident, I would ride again. Maybe most people would swear off the "deathtraps" for good after they go through as much pain and as many surgeries as I have, but it wasn't the bike's fault I got hurt. It was the drunk driver who has served his time and paid for his mistake — in more ways than one. I wasn't entirely surprised seven years ago when I heard that Chase had gotten arrested for beating the man nearly to death the day he was released from his three-year prison sentence.

While I considered going over to have dinner with my parents tonight, I just feel like being alone after the cramped plane ride home. I know they're not exactly thrilled with the idea of me leaving here to travel the world, reporting from war zones and all other types of dangerous places, but they'll still support me, like they've always done. I don't know what I would do without my parents always being there for me. After the accident, I even felt guilty for worrying them during my "rebellious phase", as they called it. They all but chanted, "Told you so" every day that Chase was absent in the hospital, and I hated admitting to myself that they were right about him all along.

Traffic isn't bad on the highway now that the sun is starting to set, so it doesn't take long to get home. I pull my car into the garage and then try to decide what frozen dinner I'll be making tonight. They all suck, but I have to watch my weight or people will start asking me on Facebook if I'm pregnant.

God, sometimes I wonder if being in the spotlight is worth the trouble.

The first stop is my bedroom where I change into a pair of blue pajama pants and a white tank top, relieved to take off my bra. Then, I head back to the kitchen to pop my calorie-controlled meal into the microwave and then grab a bottle of wine from the pantry to celebrate my successful interview with myself.

When I turn around and come face to face with a bearded man sitting as still as a statue at my counter, I scream so loudly I temporarily go deaf.

And like an idiot, my fingers lose the grip on the bottle of wine. My one and only weapon at this moment falls to the floor and shatters on the tile.

"Hi, Sasha," the man says calmly. Running his hand over his beard, he says, "You need to get better locks."

Standing there frozen, all I can do is stare at him. Automatic bodily functions like breathing have ceased to exist. And I'm utterly speechless as to why this random man would be sitting in my house like he's a welcome guest.

"Fuck!" he exclaims before he suddenly jumps up and starts around the counter toward me. He's even bigger when he's standing, well over six feet tall with thick, tattooed arms and a massive chest that makes me certain he could easily snap me in half. "You're gonna cut your feet on the glass," he says in his deep, grumbly voice as he reaches for me.

"S-stay the fuck away from me!" I warn him when my voice decides to work again as I start walking backward.

"Stop moving!" he shouts before softening his voice. "You're standing on glass, sweetheart. I shouldn't have snuck in, but I didn't exactly think you would invite me in if I came to the front door."

His voice is familiar, especially the term of endearment. And then there are his eyes that are a soft green like ferns, that aren't looking at me maliciously but with affection.

"*Chase?*" I ask aloud.

"Oh, fuck. You just *now* recognized me? Wow. Okay. Sorry," he says, running his hand over the beard again and stroking it several times like it's a nervous habit. "Guess I do look a little different with the beard, huh?"

"What the fuck are you doing in my house? How did you get in here?" I demand as my chest heaves up and down in fear, shock, and anger at him standing here in my kitchen, talking to me so normally, like he never fucking destroyed me.

...

Chase

God, I had forgotten how gorgeous Sasha was in person. The camera lens doesn't do her any justice. Although, I do miss the point of her chin and nose from before they were altered with surgery because of the accident. I really hate that my phone with all the pictures of her on it was crushed that night, leaving me with nothing but my memories of the old Sasha from my past.

And she doesn't seem nearly as glad to see me as I am to see her.

"You need better locks," I tell her again when she asks how I got in. "The back door was a piece of cake with a credit card. You need, like, deadbolts and chains and shit. Something to at least slow a burglar down while you grab a gun."

"What?" she asks, her voice shaking. "You...you're standing here, in my kitchen, talking about how *easy* it was to break into my house?" Her face begins to turn red with fury. "What I *need* is to not have some asshole barging in without my consent! And you...you of all people have some nerve coming here!"

"Slow down, sweetheart," I tell her. "This visit isn't about us or the past."

"Oh really?" she asks, crossing her arms over her chest. My eyes are drawn to where her nipples are poking through her top clear as a bell, because she's not wearing a bra.

Fuck me.

Focus, Chase!

"Can we go talk in the living room where we're not stepping on glass?" I ask, gesturing down at her bare feet that are standing in puddles of red wine with shards of glass just inches away from cutting her up.

"No!" she exclaims. "We don't need to talk! You need to get the fuck out of my house!" she yells before she turns toward the sink and grabs some paper towels.

"At least let me clean this mess up since it was my fault," I tell her.

"No. I'll clean up while you show yourself out," Sasha huffs. Squatting down with the whole roll and giving me a clear view right down her top, she starts spreading the towels out to try and soak up the red wine. The fact that it looks like blood covering her feet and hands sends me right back to the night of the wreck.

Shaking my head to clear those thoughts, I tell her, "Look, I just came by to tell you that you need to keep your nose out of that shit that went down the other day."

Pausing in her cleanup, she leaves the towels alone and stands up straight. "It *was* you, wasn't it? You caused that wreck. You killed a man!"

I fucking hate how her blue eyes look wary of me, seeing me as the bad guy I am, rather than the man she once loved.

"You don't need to worry about that. This is some dangerous shit, Sasha," I warn her.

She crosses her arms over her chest again and says, "I can't believe you and the Savage Kings are dealing the meth that's killing people. You should be ashamed of yourself, Chase Fury!"

"What?" I say in surprise. "We're not dealing shit. The Kings are trying to keep it out of our city."

"Don't lie to me, okay? You *are* dealing, and I have proof."

"What proof? What do you know?" I ask. "Tell me everything you've found out, then I want you to leave this shit alone and go back to reporting about the sand castle competitions, or what the fuck ever fluff pieces."

"Hector Cruz is the meth kingpin for the whole east coast, and I'm pretty sure that those guys you shot at...that guy you *killed*, worked for him. There's also the photos I have of Torin meeting with Hector..."

"Bullshit," I say since I don't believe that for a second. The only drug the MC deals in is weed, and soon that shit will be legal. We have a hard and fast rule about not touching any of the hard stuff.

"Really, Chase? I tell you I have photos, and you still think I'm lying?"

"No, I didn't say you were lying," I clarify. Fuck, I love hearing her say my name again, more than I should. "You're misinformed or got the wrong guy. You've never even met Torin."

"You're right. Maybe it was one of the other presidents of the Savage Kings. We all make mistakes. So, how about I get my phone and show you the photos to let you see for yourself?"

"Yes, let me see them so I can tell you that you're wrong," I tell her, having no doubts that she is mistaken on this.

"Even Jade admitted it was Torin. She said she was going to talk to him about it," Sasha informs me.

Motherfucker. I guess Torin left that part out of our meeting.

"Go get the phone," I snap at her, because I can't fucking take her standing in all this glass any longer while throwing around accusations about my brother. My brother, the former Army corporal who lives and breathes being on the right side of the law whenever fucking possible. But if it was a Savage King meeting with Hector, the club needs to know who, so we can beat his ass into the ground for breaking one of our rules.

"Wow, you've really upped the asshole attitude over the years," Sasha says with a shake of her blonde head before she tiptoes out of the kitchen and disappears down a hallway.

While she's gone, I gather up all the red soaked towels and shards of glass and toss them in the trash can next to the counter. The mess is only halfway clean when Sasha comes back into the room with her phone.

"Wait over there," I tell her when I see her in the doorway. She rolls her eyes but actually listens, waiting for me to come to her.

"Here," she says when I'm right in front of her, the closest I've been able to get in a decade. When her cute button nose wrinkles in revulsion, I know she's smelling the cigarette smoke on me and still disapproves of the habit, making me want to quit cold turkey. And how is it that she stills smells exactly the same, that sweet apple scent making my mouth water? You'd think by now I would've gotten over her, stopped wanting her, but it's the exact opposite. I'd give anything to touch her. But, knowing she's not a fan of the idea, I keep my hands to myself and look down to take the phone from her.

That's when I see it...my name, written in small, black cursive letters that have started to fade.

"I, ah, I thought you had that removed," I tell her, barely refraining from touching the ink.

"What?" she asks, then looks down at her outstretched hand. "Oh." Seeing it, she slaps her other hand over the letters.

"L-laser removal surgery isn't cheap," she says, then clears her throat, which was always her tell for when she was lying.

"No shit?" I reply since I've never looked into it. The Kings make damn good money, so even if it cost six figures, I could afford it. Not that I would remove her name from my skin even if I could. "It never shows on camera," I point out.

"You watch?" Sasha asks, her blue eyes widening in surprise.

"Every night."

"Oh," she says, looking away as her cheeks begin to redden again. "Well, WBRL *is* the most popular network in the area."

Because you're on it, I withhold.

"They have this special makeup for tattoos to cover them," she explains.

"Now I know," I reply with a grin as hope blooms in my cold, dead heart.

Sasha's parents are loaded. Her father owns several car dealerships, not the shady used car kind but the hot off the factory line ones. Removing my name from her body after the accident would've been high on their to-do list. Hell, I assumed it was high on hers, but she kept it. She kept a piece of me with her. If I had known that when I first started watching her on camera six years ago, I would've been ecstatic and probably came to see her then. Stupid fucking makeup.

"Anyway," Sasha says with a shake of her head. "Here." When the screen of her phone goes black, she presses a few buttons to bring up the image again and then offers it to me. What were we talking about again? Oh, right. The man she *thinks* is Torin.

I take the device from her and bring it closer to my face.

"Son of a bitch!" I exclaim. Using my finger and thumb to zoom in on the photo, I get a real good look at my brother wearing his cut, leaning against a brick building next to the greasy bastard that I recognize as the meth king of the east coast, who I'm sure the Aces distribute for.

"Goddamn," I mutter as I scrub my left hand down my face.

Why didn't I put it together before? That day I put a beatin' on Johnny, the Aces bartender must have called Hector and told him Abe and I were at the bar about to leave. He sicced those assholes on us. And my brother...what part does he play in all of this?

"So it is Torin?" Sasha asks, her blue eyes sparkling with triumph.

"Yes," I admit, since she already figured out as much.

"And you didn't know about him meeting with Cruz?"

"Hell no," I grumble. "The Kings don't have shit to do with meth."

"So just your brother does?" Sasha suggests.

"No! Fuck, no. Torin's got an old lady and a kid on the way. He wouldn't touch the stuff for himself or for profit. The MC makes plenty of money for him to support them. He probably has millions in the bank, so why..."

I realize I'm saying all this shit aloud as I think through it.

"You may be an asshole, but I'm sorry that you had to find out this way," Sasha says.

My mind's reeling, my thoughts going in a million different directions. So what if there's a photo with Torin and a drug kingpin? That doesn't mean Torin is dealing or buying or selling for him. They could've just been hanging out. Although, that doesn't make sense either...

"When was this taken?" I ask, as I forward the picture to myself to have a copy, and to save Sasha's number.

"Yesterday," she replies.

"Maybe Torin was there bitching Hector out for the three overdoses," I suggest, thinking that's the more likely scenario.

Sasha clears her throat to get my attention, which isn't hard.

"What?" I ask.

"Keep scrolling," she tells me. "There are more photos."

I swipe left to pull up the next photo. "Mother. Fucker."

Torin is handing Hector an armful of stacks of cash about five times larger than the fifteen thousand stack that I got from the Aces.

In the next photo, Torin's looking around as if worried about someone seeing him while Hector and his men counts the money.

"Jesus fucking Christ!" I exclaim as I clench the phone in my fist. Before I break the damn thing, I forward the other pictures to myself. When I get to a selfie of Sasha and her dad I hand it back to her.

"You can't go public with this," I warn her.

Spine straightening and sticking her tits out, she shouts, "The hell I can't! I'm a reporter; this is what I do!"

"If you don't back off of this, you're gonna get hurt!"

"Worse than *you* hurt me?" she replies, her eyes beginning to shimmer.

There's no pain as brutal as having that particular truth thrown back at me. It feels like she took the knife from my belt and carved out my heart with it.

Hell, I deserve it.

"You're right, I did hurt you, and I've suffered the worst possible punishment for it, knowing that you'll never fucking forgive me..."

"No, I won't," she agrees, wrapping her arms protectively around herself.

"And that even after all this time it's impossible for me to stop loving you –"

The last word barely leaves my mouth before her palm connects with my face. The resounding *WHAP* echoes through the otherwise silent house.

"You don't get to say those words to me," Sasha seethes as her chest rises and falls in anger.

Reaching up, I run my fingertips over the unexpected but deserved sting on my cheek that her hand left behind. "Why not?" I ask. "They're the truth."

"Don't!" she shouts, her blue eyes fierce and glowing. "Don't you *fucking* dare...not after what you did to me. Get the fuck out of my house!"

She still cares about me. Hell, now I even think she still loves me. Nothing invokes that sort of physical response from such a sweet woman except for hate. Hate because she wishes she could erase me from her mind, her heart, her skin...but she can't, even though she's tried. It's hard to hate someone unless you loved them, and they hurt you beyond repair.

I turn away from her to let her cool down, but I don't leave. Instead, I go back over to the mess on the floor and finish cleaning it up so that Sasha won't have to risk cutting herself.

After a minute or two, Sasha clears her throat, warning me that a lie is coming. "If you don't leave, I'll call the police."

Since my back is to her, I smile, knowing she can't see it. "What are you gonna tell them?" I ask without looking at her. "That some asshole broke into your house and started cleaning?"

She blows out a huffy breath behind me because she knows that I'm onto her, and I remember when she's obviously bluffing.

"I'll, um," small throat clearing and stammering, letting me know a doozy is coming. "I'll tell the police that you killed that guy in the SUV."

Tossing a pile of wine-soaked towels into the trash, I look over at her and say, "Try again, sweetheart. You're gonna have to be a little more convincing than that."

I wet some paper towels in the sink and then squat down to wipe up the last of the stickiness on the floor.

"Sergeant Barnes of the Highway Patrol is on my speed dial. Should I call him?" Sasha asks, making me freeze. She didn't stammer or clear her throat. She's telling the truth, and I...I fucking hate it.

"You *should* call him," I lie through my clenched jaw when I stand up to toss the wet towels on the counter before facing her. "Because if you're trying to make me jealous, it'd be much more effective if you knew his first fucking name."

Her front teeth bite down into her bottom lip when she realizes her mistake. "I'm done, so I'll show myself out. Be sure to lock up behind me," I tell her with a wink before I stroll over and walk out the back door.

Once it shuts, I stand there a minute. Unable to leave her without another glance, I look over my shoulder to get a final glimpse of her. She didn't follow me to lock the door. Instead, her back slides down the wall until her ass hits the floor. Then, she buries her face in her hands.

I know she's crying, and I wish I could hold her and make it better, but that's not what she wants from me or what I can give her.

Ten years ago, I hurt her beyond repair. There's nothing I can do or say to make her forgive me.

Finally, I force my boots to take me to my bike that I stowed in a parking lot a few blocks over, comforting myself with the fact that this won't be the last time I see her.

Sasha's stubborn with a wild side that's drawn to danger. She won't give up on the Torin and Hector bullshit, which means I'm not gonna take my eyes off her.

CHAPTER EIGHT

Sasha

"IT'S IMPOSSIBLE FOR ME TO STOP LOVING YOU."

"Ughhh!" I scream as I slap my trembling hands over my ears, as if that will stop the words from repeating like a broken record in my head. One of my palms is still burning from hitting Chase. I shouldn't have done that, but I couldn't stand there and listen to him lie to my face.

How? How can he say those words to me? If he loved me, he wouldn't have run. He would've been by my side when I woke up in the hospital, holding my hand, and telling me that everything was going to be fine.

A sob rips from my throat as the pain of being abandoned by the one person I thought I could count on comes roaring back.

God, I loved Chase so much. I worshipped the ground he walked on, so his sudden absence in my life without a single explanation fucking destroyed me. My scars and his name on my wrist are the constant reminders of the agony I went through, coming to terms with the fact that the man I loved didn't really love me, at least not enough to stay with me through the surgeries and recovery.

And I fucking hate that, even though we haven't spoken in years, he could tell when I was lying to him. How is that possible? It doesn't make sense. Neither does the idea of him watching me on the news every night. Was he serious? That stupid notion shouldn't fill my stomach with butterflies. It doesn't matter if he watches me or if he breaks into my house and cleans up shit. Not *once* has he apologized to me or explained why he gave up on us.

In my heart, I never gave up on him. That's why I haven't been able to get his name erased from my body. I've gone to the tattoo removal office at least three times, mostly at my father's urging, and once when I was first hired at WRBL because they insisted I remove the ink as part of my contract. All three times I left before I even finished the consultation appointment. The studio gave up fighting me on it once I showed them that I could cover it with makeup dark enough to prevent the black letters from appearing on camera.

But seeing Chase tonight, knowing that he's the one who killed a man and hurt two others on the highway and is into no telling what else with the MC, it's time for me to finally put the past behind me. Hopefully, I'll hear from the network in D.C. with a job offer soon.

Until then, I need to quit clinging to the past, to a man I don't even know, and who I still question if he ever cared about me at all.

I don't know why he showed up here and said those things when his main purpose was apparently to warn me to stay away from Hector and the MC. But letting this story go is not going to happen, especially not because he asked.

Does Chase think that I won't turn him into the police because of our history? He didn't seem to believe me when I made the threat to try to get him to leave. But I don't owe any loyalty to him. He lost that years ago. Now my safety and my career come first.

I'm not naïve enough to think that Chase wouldn't hurt me if it meant him or everyone in his club going to prison.

Glancing at the phone that I dropped next to me on the floor, I pick it up with a shaky hand and go to my text messages, typing out a new one because I'm too upset to try and speak to anyone right now.

The response is instantaneous.

Leaning my head back against the wall, I tell myself that this decision is the smartest one for my safety and even my sanity.

If only I could get my heart to agree...

...

Chase

Being in the same room with Sasha, seeing her and getting to be so close to her has my head spinning as I ride back to the clubhouse.

Thinking of how tough she is makes me smile with pride, knowing that she's learned how to stand up for herself. When we were teenagers, she would always back down when her father chewed her out or her mom raised hell at her; and I always told her to hold her ground with them because it was time for them to stop treating her like a child.

She really fucking hates me, though, which I deserve. I just wasn't expecting her ferocity. And fuck, it was hot when she slapped me. I want her to yell at me, hit me, kick me, scratch my eyeballs out. Hell, she could do anything she wanted to work her anger out on me, and I'd let her. I know a better, more enjoyable physical outlet for her, but I doubt she would be interested. *Yet.*

If she still loves me enough to loathe me so violently, then maybe I can find a way to convince her to give me another chance.

After the wreck, Sasha said she never wanted to see me again; and I gave her space, knowing I had caused her enough pain. I didn't think it was fair to keep harassing her or begging her to forgive me. So, I let her have the one thing she needed at the time — me out of her life, even though I needed her so fucking bad.

Maybe this shit with Torin was fate's way of giving us a second chance. I *won't* fuck it up.

Sasha's set on getting in the middle of some serious heat, despite my warning. If anything, that probably just got her even more interested in digging, because that girl always did love a dangerous challenge. Nothing got her hotter than when I would take her for a walk on the wild side with me. She loved the thrill, the adrenaline rush as much as I did, which is why we were so fucking perfect together.

When I pull up at *Savage Asylum*, I spot my brother getting on his bike at the other end of the lot.

"Yo, Torin!" I call out to get his attention as I park and scramble off my bike.

"What's up?" he shouts back. "I'm finally headed home, Chase. Can this wait?" he asks when I approach him, still straddling his bike.

"No."

When I'm close enough that no one else can overhear us, I say, "Why the fuck did you meet with Hector Cruz?"

Torin's eyes lower and his jaw ticks before he answers, letting me know he's pissed that I found out about that shit. What can I say? I'm fucking awesome at reading people.

"Who told you about that?" he asks, rather than give me an explanation.

"Don't worry about it."

"Was it that goddamn reporter?" he snaps. Pointing his finger at me, he says, "You need to shut her up, or I will."

Stepping forward to get in his face so close that his finger digs into my chest, I warn him, "You're not gonna do *shit* to her!"

"Back the fuck up. Now," Torin demands through gritted teeth.

I stare him down for several more seconds before I finally take a step back, my hands balled into fists at my sides.

"Look, if my name gets splattered across the evening news, it's not good for us, the MC, and definitely not Kennedy. You fucking know that, Chase, so just get the woman to stand down," he says. "Do you want to know what I was doing with Hector? I was warning him to keep his crank out of our city. Oh, and I told him that the next time someone pointed a gun at one of my men, I'd unload one in his face."

Goddamnit. He's lying right to my fucking face.

"That's it, huh? Nothing else?" I ask, hoping he'll explain why he was paying Hector stacks of money.

"That's it," he lies instead of owning up to anything. "So, do I have your word that you'll shut this shit down for good?" he asks.

"Yeah, brother," I agree as I back away from his bike and start to head into the bar.

My guess is that Sasha will be diving into this shitstorm headfirst tomorrow, despite my warning. Actually, definitely in spite of my warning, just to show me that I don't have any say over what she does.

Boy, is she wrong about that, because wherever the hell she goes, I'm going from now on.

And fuck, I could really use a smoke right now. But when I pull out the pack from the inside pocket of my cut, I look at the damn thing a minute before I toss them into the garbage can just outside the bar with a heavy sigh. I'm still just as pussy whipped as I was ten years ago, not wanting to smell like smoke because I know Sasha hates it.

"Hey, Chase," Nikki says when she comes up to me as soon as I step into the bar.

"What's up?" I ask.

"You wanna finish what we started the other night?"

Fuck no.

The response nearly explodes out of my mouth without any thought. But it's the truth. After seeing Sasha tonight, Nikki naked on my bed spread eagle wouldn't be half as appealing as Sasha in her pajamas without a bra.

"How about you take care of one of my brothers tonight?" I suggest rather than turn her down flat.

Without waiting for her response, I head to the basement and go straight to my apartment. I consider looking for Abe, but I just can't show him or anyone else the photos of Torin, his president, going against the fucking club. Once I do, then my brother will lose all of his respect, and it could ruin us.

CHAPTER NINE

Sasha

"Hi, thanks for meeting with me, Sergeant," I tell him when I approach the two-person table on the patio at *Darren's* dock-side restaurant. It's almost nine o'clock, so it's dark out, but they have lights wrapped around every rail to give it a nice romantic glow.

Sergeant Barnes stands up from his chair with a broad smile. "Call me Travis, please. It's good to see you again, Sasha." When he leans forward to hug me in greeting, I'm only a little surprised. I mean, I did send him a message asking if he could meet me for a late dinner tonight.

After we separate, I take a seat, setting my purse down beside me before I start glancing over the menu since I'm not sure what to say. While my main reason for wanting to meet tonight was to see if the Highway Patrol has any new information about the accident and the MC, I know I should be excited about having dinner with a hand-some man.

Unfortunately, the spark of attraction for more than friendship just isn't there, and I doubt it ever will be.

Fucking Chase Fury.

A waitress comes to take our drink order, and I go ahead and give her my entrée choice too, trying to speed things along.

"So," I start once we're alone again. "How's the, um, the case going for that highway seventeen accident?" I ask.

"Oh," Travis replies as his shoulders slump slightly. "Am I on the record? Because I thought this was –"

"Sorry to put you on the spot," I tell him with a smile. "I'm sure the mind of the reporter isn't much different from an officer's, always thinking about work."

There, I didn't admit or deny that this isn't a date. To get dirt, sometimes you have to venture into muddy water. And if flirting with the man a little tonight can get me some information about Hector or the Kings, then it'll be worth it.

"Right," Travis says. "We haven't identified any suspects."

"Oh, no? That's too bad," I tell him, reaching over to give his forearm a light pat and leaving it resting there.

"Yeah, well, we didn't have enough evidence to ask every member of the Savage Kings to come in for a lineup, and of course, it could've been someone wearing one of their cuts that doesn't have any ties to the MC."

"Right," I agree, trying not to sound relieved.

"You're familiar with the MC, though, aren't you?" Travis asks.

"Excuse me?" I reply, trying not to let the truth show on my face.

"After your outburst at the scene, I looked you up in the system," he answers with a smirk. "Your, ah, accident when you were a teenager? Well, I'm guessing Fury was only a prospect at the time, but you had to have known he had ties to the MC, right?"

"Wh-I don't know what you're talking about," I lie, and it's not even the least bit convincing to my own ears. Shit.

"Chase Fury? From what we hear, he's now the vice president of the original Savage Kings charter. You two must have been close since he has your name tattooed on his chest."

"How...how did you know that?" I ask.

"All of his tattoos are listed on his arrest record from the aggravated assault about, what was it? Six, seven years back? That time he took a crowbar to both of the drunk driver's knees the same day the guy was released from prison for hitting the two of you."

"Wow," I mutter as I reach for the glass of water in front of me to take a sip. My mouth has gone as dry as the desert. Chase took out the guy's *knees*? I knew he went to prison for assaulting him, but I was in college then, trying to stay focused on getting over a broken heart and getting my degree, so I never knew any of the details. "You've certainly done your homework," I tell Travis.

"Has he contacted you?"

"What? God, no!" I exclaim, a little too loudly for being out in public. Glancing around nervously, I have to clear my throat before I can say, "I-I haven't seen...Chase since the night of the accident."

Saying his name out loud is still hard for me.

"He's dangerous," Travis says simply, like that's breaking news. "And he matches the description of the highway shooter, so I wouldn't be surprised if we find enough evidence to bring him into the station for questioning on a first degree murder and two felony attempted murder charges. If we do, he probably won't ever walk out again."

"Right, of course," I agree with a nod. "That's awful what happened out there, even if it did happen to three known meth dealers connected to Hector Cruz."

"Cruz is even more dangerous than Fury," Travis tells me. "You don't want to mess with him or start reporting his business on the six o'clock news."

"As an officer of the law, you don't think the police should be looking into bringing down one of the biggest drug kingpins on the east coast?"

Picking up his glass of water, Travis shrugs his shoulders. "I'm just a highway patrolman. All I'm worried about are the assholes on the road."

Wow. I'm getting a really bad feeling about this guy. And now, I'm regretting asking him to meet me tonight.

...

Chase

WHILE I MAY LOOK like a creepy stalker, watching a woman on a date with a man through a pair of binoculars, I'm really just trying to keep Sasha safe.

I'd rather gouge my eyeballs out than see another man wrap his arms around her or watch her having a romantic dinner with him on the dock. That should've been me sitting there across from her.

From what I can tell, even though the fucking place is dimly lit, I'm pretty sure she's with the trooper bastard that she mentioned last night.

Why would she agree to go out on a date with him tonight, when she didn't even know his first name yesterday?

I don't know what Sasha's up to, but I would like to think that she's just seeing him to get more information about the shit I told her to stay out of, rather than consider that she's interested in the asshole.

He's not her type anyway.

My girl would be bored out of her goddamn mind if she had to spend her life with some straight-ass dickhead cop who doesn't know how to have a good time by breaking a few rules now and then. And the son of a bitch definitely wouldn't be able to keep her happy in the bedroom.

Sasha was a wildcat. While she would pretend like she was worried about getting caught, I knew she would rather fuck me in public than in a bed. My bike was just one of the places we hit. There were several places around the school and town where we left wet spots.

I'm guessing Howdy fucking Doody over there wouldn't do it anywhere except his bedroom with the lights off, missionary style.

Not that I want him and Sasha to end up there tonight, even if I do know she would hate every goddamn second.

After what feels like forever but is probably only fifteen minutes, Sasha stands up and walks away from the table with her purse. I spot her coming out the front door a second later and know for a fact that they haven't even brought out their food yet.

I nearly chuckle out loud at the sucker's bad luck, but since my truck windows are rolled down to let some air in, I keep quiet. My bike is too damn loud and noticeable, so for my surveillance to work, it's my truck tonight. I slouch down in my seat when Sasha starts for the parking lot. She climbs into her classic Mustang, the same one she had in high school that she and her dad rebuilt, and drives away.

Once she's out on the road, I reach for the key to crank the engine and follow her, but then I see the fucking cop headed my way, so I stay put. He's got his cell phone up to his ear and a scowl on his face.

I bet he's calling his mommy to let her know he won't be bringing Sasha home to meet her anytime soon. His voice drifts through the wind as he gets closer.

"He broke a man's knees and went to prison for over a year for her. She's your best bet at drawing him away from the MC where he'll be unprotected."

Son. Of. A. Bitch.

Is he fucking saying what I think he is?

"But you can't hurt her. She's a local celebrity. If she goes missing, every asshole up and down the coast will be looking for her. Follow her and wait for Fury to show. Fine! Give it a few days. But if you have to grab her, then do it quietly at her house; then set up the meet. I don't know! Have her call the clubhouse for him?" he says before he slips into his Mercedes.

And if every fucking thing I just overheard didn't send up warning flags, a trooper driving an expensive ride like that sure would. They don't get paid enough for something that fancy. Travis is on someone's payroll; and if I had to guess based on his phone call, it's Hector's.

The Aces at that bar must have told Hector I was there, so he knows I killed his men. And Travis must have found Sasha's connection to me from her accident report years ago.

From what I heard, the bottom line is that Hector wants to use Sasha to get me alone and put a bullet through my skull for revenge.

Does Torin know? He and Hector seem to be buddies, so why wouldn't he give him a heads-up that I'm on his shit list?

This asshole cop and I need to have a talk.

If I had to bet, I'm guessing he'll be on standby waiting for the call from Hector, telling them I'm dead so that he can swoop in and be there for Sasha. She doesn't need him, and I'll never let that fucking happen.

But I can't exactly blow his head off either. I don't need any more heat on me.

CHAPTER TEN

Sasha

After my surprise visitor last night, I can't help but be a little jumpy when I pull into my garage and get out of my car.

While I told Chase to leave, I don't expect that to be the last I see of him.

The anxiety that's swirling around my empty stomach is simultaneously accompanied by a tiny sliver of, dare I admit it, *hope.*

Hope is such a stupid fucking emotion. I should know by now that all it leads to is devastation.

I already have my house key out of my purse and in my hand to put in the front door. I forgot to leave the porch light on when I went to work, and it's too dark to easily find the keyhole. I'm sure I've got it lined up straight; but no matter how I manipulate it, I can't seem to get the key to slide all the way in.

Pulling out my cell phone to use as a flashlight, I shine it on the lock and try again.

Well, there is the problem. My key just doesn't fit.

What the hell?

I look through the keys on my ring, one for my office at work, one for my car, one for my parents' house, and finally my house. Just to make sure I'm not losing my mind, I try them all but get nowhere.

Deciding that the lock is jammed from the humidity or something, I start to turn around and go try the back door, when my phone light lands on a black box with a red ribbon sitting on the porch.

Since it's not my birthday or any other holiday, my first thought is that someone left it here by mistake. Stepping closer, I see my name penned messily on a white tag that has to be a man's handwriting.

If I had to guess, I would even say it's from a man with a beard who wears leather and rides a Harley.

Too curious to resist, I bend down and pick it up, then fumble around in the dark, trying to unwrap it with my keys and phone in my one hand.

I pull off the lid and find a shiny gold key lying on a pillow of white cotton.

Seriously?

Of course, the key slides right into the lock on my front door. Both of the locks, I notice when the door doesn't open after the first one.

A second later and I'm finally inside my house that now has two shiny gold deadbolts to match the key.

I can't believe he broke into my house again and changed my locks!

It's hard to feel safer when I know that Chase no doubt also has a key. Now he won't even have to break in!

Turning on the lights as I walk through the house, making sure he's not lurking around, I stop in the kitchen where I find another gift – a bottle of wine, just like the one I dropped yesterday with a bow tied around it too.

There's a handwritten note on a torn-out sheet of notebook paper in front of it that says, "Next time I'll call to tell you I'm coming."

That...asshole!

Why did he have to go and do something sweet when I'm trying my best to keep hating him? I *have* to hate him. Otherwise, he'll just hurt me again. I don't know if my heart can be glued back together again. It's already pretty weak as it is.

...

THE NEXT DAY AT WORK, the station is buzzing, people running around frantically like when it's a big news day as soon I walk through the door around four-thirty to start my hair and makeup. Since I spent the morning fishing with my dad, I haven't had the news on.

"What's going on around here?" I ask Chelsea, our hairstylist, when I sit down in her chair.

"You haven't heard?" she asks with her eyes widening, and I shake my head. "There was a drowning."

"And?" I ask, since drownings are, unfortunately, a pretty normal occurrence in a coastal town during the summer.

"And it was some Highway Patrol guy."

"Really?" I ask as cold dread spreads through the blood in my veins. "Who? What was his name?"

"I can't remember," Chelsea says. "I wanna say Barrett or Bates or..."

"Barnes?" I ask as I swallow around the gigantic knot in my throat.

Snapping her fingers, she says, "Yep, that's the one. How did you guess?"

"Just lucky that way," I tell her as my stomach bottoms out and my fingers start to tremble.

"Are you okay?" she asks. "You look a little pale, Sash."

"I-I'm not feeling well, actually." As if saying the words were a call to action, I jump up and push Chelsea aside to heave and toss my cookies into her trash bin.

Oh my god, Chase! What did you do now?

"Jeez, girl. Are you okay?" she asks from behind me, then offers me some tissues that I appreciate, using them to wipe my mouth. Gasping, Chelsea says, "You're not pregnant, are you?"

"No. God, no," I tell her with a shake of my head as I straighten and turn to face her. "What do they know...about the drowning? Was there...foul play?" I ask as I force down another lurch of my stomach.

"No," she replies with her brow furrowed.

"There wasn't?" I ask in disbelief.

It had to have been Chase! Did he follow me last night after he changed my locks? Did he kill Travis because he thought we were on a date? Oh God, what have I done?

"No, the guy hit his head or something," she informs me. "Medical examiner said he must have gone for a night swim and smashed his head when he dived into the shallow end or whatever. It was a horrible accident."

A horrible accident named Chase fucking Fury.

"There weren't any other wounds on him?" I ask.

Chelsea stares at me like she's starting to think I'm insane. "I don't think so, but I didn't memorize the entire article."

"Sorry," I tell her. "It's just, well, I went on a date with Travis last night."

"Oooh, who's Travis?" she asks, her eyes sparkling with interest.

"Barnes. Travis is Travis Barnes, the guy who..."

"Ohhh!" she replies as her jaw drops. "God, Sasha. I'm so sorry." She wraps me in a hug that I accept because I need someone to hold me together right now.

This is bad. Really bad.

There were a ton of people at *Darren's* last night who saw us sitting together. I need to go to the police before they come to me wondering why I didn't speak up and say something. And I want to hear all of the facts of his death straight from them.

CHAPTER ELEVEN

Chase

Once I made sure Sasha was safe and sound asleep in her bed last night, I got Reece, the MC's tech guy, to find me an address for the trooper fucker. Then, I found him climbing out of the luxurious pool out behind his enormous house he couldn't afford on a cop's salary. All I wanted to do was have a little chat with him, but then he charged me. The two of us ended up grappling right before we fell into the pool and Howdy Doody busted his skull on the bottom. He was already floating face down when I climbed out of the pool soaking wet and made a run for it.

I didn't want to kill him. I just wanted to make him tell me what Hector and Torin were up to before I kicked his ass and warned him to stay away from Sasha.

Still, I'm not sad that the asshole is gone. The dumbass could've gotten Sasha killed.

I got a few hours of sleep while Sasha was fishing with her dad, but I'm fucking beat. It's almost nine o'clock at night, and she still hasn't gone home yet. First, she went to the news station, then the police department. Since then, I've been a little on edge, worried that she might try and finger me for killing the trooper. But she wasn't in there long before she was headed back to the news station only looking a little upset.

Finally, she finished up her night and drove back to her house.

I'm about to doze off when I see movement at the front of the house. Sasha struts toward her car in...I squint my eyes to look closer through the windshield, then grab the binoculars from the passenger seat to look through them.

Is she wearing leather pants? And I swear only two strings are holding up her thin top.

No fucking way.

Where in the hell is she going?

I'm on my phone calling her before I even think twice.

"Hello?" she answers from the driver's seat of her car.

"Where the hell are you going dressed like that?" I snap.

"So you *are* watching the house," she says. "We need to talk."

"Then why didn't you just call me, sweetheart?" I ask, since my number's in her phone from forwarding the photos the other night.

"Don't call me that," she huffs. "I'm not your sweetheart, or anything else."

"Sure, sweetheart," I say, just to get her good and riled up.

"Chase!" she shouts. And then, in a hushed whisper, she asks, "Did you kill him?"

"You'll have to be more specific. Who are we talking about?" I hedge.

"Chase."

If she says my name whenever she's pissed, then I'll make sure she's always mad at me.

"Did you?"

"That requires more than a yes or no answer," I say as I watch her turning around to look over her shoulder. "It was an accident. But serves the fucker right. He was on Hector's payroll."

"You're lying! Were you jealous? Is that why you did it?" she asks.

"He was on Hector's payroll," I say again slowly, rather than admit that I was jealous seeing them together. "And I overheard him telling Hector to use you to get to me. Sasha, they were gonna kidnap you and do no telling what if I didn't show up in a few days."

"What?" she gasps into the phone, searching over her shoulder again.

"There's a black Mazda out your driveway and to the right parked in front of that brick house with the red mailbox," I tell her. "They've been watching you all day."

"Shit!" she exclaims.

"I'm over on the left, watching them watch you."

"All day?" she asks.

"Yep."

"What are we gonna do?" she asks. And I've never loved the word *we* more than I do right fucking now. It means she's giving me an in with her, letting me take care of her.

"I've got an idea," I tell her. "You're not gonna like it."

"I'm scared," she whispers, and hearing the fear in her voice fucking guts me.

Squeezing my eyes shut to take a deep breath, I tell her, "It's gonna be fine, sweetheart. I've got you."

"Okay," she agrees, trusting me to keep her safe now even though I let her down before.

"You still remember how to shoot a gun?" I ask.

"Yes. But I don't have –"

"There's one under the top left of your mattress, loaded and ready. And another one in the pantry behind the sugar."

"Why couldn't you be romantic and leave flowers instead of firearms?" she jokes, even though I can still hear the fear behind her words.

"Because I'm trying to keep you safe," I tell her. "And flowers never made your heart race or your panties wet."

"Chase!" she chastises me, even though she knows it's true.

"Get out of your car and go back inside. Leave the front door unlocked. Grab the gun from the mattress and hide in the bathroom until I say it's safe to come out."

"What are you going to do?" she asks.

"Don't worry about that."

"You're going to walk right up to my door, aren't you?"

"Told you that you wouldn't like it," I reply with a grin.

Her sigh is heavy through the phone line.

"It's the fastest way to get this over with, sweetheart," I tell her honestly. "And my nerves can't take another day of them following you."

"Are you...are you going to kill them?" she asks.

"They want to kidnap you and hurt you to get to me," I remind her. "I'd kill them twice if I could."

"What about Hector?" she asks, not even trying to talk me out of harming the men or convince me that I should go to the police. That's why I fell in love with this woman. She may have been told to act like a good girl her whole life, but she was born to be a fucking outlaw.

"We'll work our way up to Hector," I tell her, using my new favorite word.

"Did you talk to Torin?" she asks.

"One problem at a time, sweetheart," I reply.

"Okay, fine," she agrees with a sigh. "I'm going inside."

"Good. I'll be right there," I assure her. "Take your phone. And if anyone other than me comes to the bathroom door, fire through it aiming at chest level, then call nine-one-one."

Ending the call, I pull out my nine and screw on the silencer, ready to get this shit done.

CHAPTER TWELVE

Sasha

Holding the small Ruger in my hand feels strange. I don't exactly enjoy handling guns, but I am familiar with them. My father took me to the gun range for the first time when I was sixteen to teach me how to shoot for protection. I liked trying to hit the bullseye on the paper sheets, but I don't think I could ever fire it at another human being.

And I don't think I'll have to make that decision tonight either.

I know Chase will take care of whoever comes after him; I just can't believe that they were going to use me to try and kill him.

When Travis started bringing up all those details about Chase and me, I should've realized that he had a reason, and it wasn't that he was just curious about my ex-boyfriend.

Travis didn't deserve to die for doing Hector's dirty work for him, but how can I be upset with Chase when I know he did it to protect me? If he says it was an accident, then I believe him.

And if Travis was on Hector's payroll, then half the local police department could be too. That means that calling them for help would only make things worse for us.

Chase made the tough decision, like he's also doing tonight.

While I would like to think that he's doing it all for me, I know he's more concerned with his own self-preservation; and I happen to benefit from his actions.

I jump when my phone vibrates on the linoleum bathroom floor beside me. Thank God I knew better than to keep my finger on the trigger of the gun or I could've accidentally pulled it when I got startled.

Picking up the phone, I read the message on the screen.

I'm outside the bathroom door. Open up and don't shoot.

I quickly type back,

How do I know someone didn't steal your phone and type this message pretending to be you?

I wait for a response, seeing the three dots moving, telling me he's typing a response.

The first time you fucked me was in the front seat of your Mustang when we were skipping third period. The first time I went down on you we were under the boardwalk. You swore it was the most religious experience you would ever have in this lifetime. Should I go on?

God, the memories that a few sentences can invoke is unreal. And my body is definitely not immune to the reminders. Even a decade later, it still remembers how good Chase made it feel and craves it again.

Replying to his message, I say,

Of course all you would remember is the sex stuff.

From the other side of the door, Chase says, "*Sweetheart, I remember every fucking thing. Every day, every second. Right now you need to pack a bag so we can get the hell out of here; but if you want, I'll spend the rest of the night proving that to you."*

Pack a bag and leave with him?

Jesus. I think I'm more terrified of doing that than I would've been if one of Hector's goons was on the other side of the door.

"*Open up*!" Chase says.

"Always so bossy," I mutter to myself.

Getting to my feet, I take a deep breath and crack open the door, leaving the gun on the linoleum.

Finding Chase sitting on the edge of my bed in his leather cut and tattered jeans like he belongs on it makes my hormones yawn and stretch their arms above their heads, like they've finally decided to wake up after a ten-year drought.

"You okay?" he asks. Standing up in front of me, he shoves his phone into his jean pocket. Then, his pale green eyes watch me with concern and worry filling them.

"Yeah," I reply, acutely aware of how that one question was all that I wanted from him after the accident, and I never got it. "Thanks for not bailing on me this time."

He lifts one of his thick reddish-blond eyebrows in question as he rubs his hand over his beard in thought. When he opens his mouth to say something, the doorbell rings.

"Who –" I start, my eyes bulging in worry.

"Calm down. It's the prospects. I've had them following me around in case I needed backup."

"What are they –"

"They're gonna clean up and watch the house."

"Clean up?" I ask, and then understanding dawns. "The, um, dead guys?"

"Yeah," Chase replies before his eyes narrow. "Look, I needed to get you out of here like ten minutes ago. Pack your shit and meet me in the living room. You've got two minutes."

"Where are we going?" I ask.

"The farmhouse," he answers, not giving me a chance to question him further before I'm left looking at the bearded skull on his jacket when he strolls out of the room.

...

Chase

"I WANT THIS PLACE SPOTLESS," I tell Maddox and Holden, our two twenty-something prospects, when I open Sasha's front door to let them in. These guys do all of our grunt work for a year or so until we vote on whether or not to patch them in.

"Did you park a few blocks over like I told you?" I ask when they come in and eye the two big bodies face down on the floor.

"Yes, sir," they both answer.

"Important lesson here, gentlemen," I say with a wave of my hand to the dead men. "These two idiots followed me into the house, just like I hoped they would. I left the door unlocked and was waiting for them behind it. One shot in the back of each head with a silencer. They never even knew they made a mistake. Make sure you never make the same one. Don't get too confident and always double-check your entryways."

"Yes, sir," they agree.

"After they're out of here and you clean up, come back and take the Mazda out front up to the salvage yard and have Eddie crush it. If they have cell phones, save them, just pull out the SIM cards. Then, I want you to lay low in the house until sunrise."

"Got it," Maddox agrees instantly, right before Holden shoots him a questioning look.

"What?" I say flatly, staring down Holden.

"Uh, it's just...Torin told us to go to Newport tomorrow. Ian called and needed money on his commissary. We were going to go visit and take care of it. One of us could go, I guess..."

"I'll get Dalton to do it," I interrupt him. Ian's got a few months left to serve after getting picked up making a run with a pound of the club's weed in his saddlebags. He kept his mouth shut and is doing his time. So, if he needs money for ramen noodles, I'll go myself, if it comes to it. "You two stay together, you hear me? These aren't likely to be the last bodies we have to deal with, so you watch out for each other."

"One more thing. Don't say a word about this to anyone, even Torin," I warn them. Both of their eyes widen and mouths drop open as if to question that. "Not. A fucking. Word," I repeat. "I'll tell Torin, but he hears it from me first. Understood?"

"Yes, sir," they answer in unison. When both of their eyes cut to the left behind me and sweep downward instantaneously, I know Sasha's finally ready.

"Don't look at her," I snap at them, and they jump before glancing away at the opposite wall. Mostly I'm just fucking with them, because that's what we do to prospects. If they patch in, they'll get to repay the favor someday. But also, I know Sasha is a fucking knockout any day, but wearing those skin-tight leather pants and flimsy shirt with no bra, she's a walking wet dream, hotter than any pin-up girl that's ever appeared in *Easy Rider* magazine.

"Oh my God," Sasha mutters when she spots the bodies. I could've stopped her before she came into the room, but I'm not gonna sugar coat shit for her. She's a tough girl and can handle it. If not, then I need to know now.

"Holden and Maddox are gonna make all this disappear," I assure her. "It won't come back on you, or we'll have two more bodies to bury," I joke.

"Do they, um, need my mop?" she asks, making me bite back my grin when the guys whip their heads around to look at her with hearts in their eyes like she's too perfect to be real. It's fucking true.

"No, sweetheart. They'll use their own cleaning supplies," I say as I go over and grab her arm to take her out the back.

"Call me if anyone parks outside the house," I tell the guys before we take the long way through the yard to my truck.

CHAPTER THIRTEEN

Sasha

"I HAVE TO GO TO WORK TOMORROW AFTERNOON," I TELL Chase, mostly just to break the silence in the cab of his truck. The small space smells too familiar, like the comforting leather scent that always lingered on him back when we were dating. Surprisingly, it doesn't smell like cigarette smoke.

Was I disappointed he wasn't on his bike? Heck yes. But I'm still shaking so badly from everything back at the house that I probably wouldn't have been able to hold on.

"We'll see," Chase replies.

"No. I have to go to work tomorrow."

"I heard you," he agrees, eyes staring straight ahead as we wind through the country roads to his parents' farmhouse. "And I said we'll see."

Rather than argue with him, I simply lean my head back against the seat to try and calm my nerves.

"Why aren't we going to the clubhouse?" I ask.

"Because Torin thinks you're a threat," he answers, surprising me with his honesty. "I don't want you near him until I figure out what he's paying Hector for."

"Did you ask him?"

"Yes," Chase replies.

"And?"

"And he lied to me. I didn't mention the money exchange to see if he'd own up to that shit. He said he was warning Hector to keep the crank out of our county."

"I'm sorry," I tell Chase. I know he and his brother are close, and it must be hard to deal with him lying. Chase missed Torin like crazy while he was in the Army. I think that's one reason he was drawn to his uncle's MC when he was so young; he wanted that brotherhood.

"It doesn't matter what the relationship is with Torin and Hector, though," he says. "Hector's not gonna back off on trying to take me out, so he's gotta go."

"Yeah," I agree. Hector's a horrible man, and if the choice is between Chase or Hector, well, I don't want anything to happen to Chase for the same reason I can't erase his name from my skin.

"Do you think more guys will show up at my house?" I ask.

Chase shrugs. "Maybe. Maybe not. I wasn't gonna sit around and wait for more bodies to pile up."

Clearing my throat, I ask, "What will your dad and stepmom say about me staying with them?"

"They don't live at the farmhouse anymore," he answers. "A few years ago, they decided they wanted to live on the beach, so they sold the house to the MC and bought a new one at Topsail Island."

"Oh," I reply in surprise. "So, who lives in the farmhouse?"

"No one," he answers.

So...does that mean, it'll just be him and me alone together tonight?

"Our grow house is in the basement. We have a few workers that tend it," he explains.

"Grow house? Like weed?"

"Yep," he replies. "It was cheaper to grow our own than buy it.

Then, when we had more than we could use, we started selling it to the other charters to bring in some extra cash."

"Oh. Well, that's not that big of a deal. It'll probably be legal soon anyway," I tell him.

"Yeah. Maybe."

The rest of our ride is in silence. After we hit the bumpy gravel road, I know we're close.

When we were together, I spent more time at Chase's dad and stepmother's than he did at my house, since they actually liked me. My parents wouldn't allow Chase to come over. They had no clue that he was sneaking into my room most nights after they went to bed.

The white, two-story house with a wraparound porch comes into the headlights view. It's completely dark, not a single light left on.

"You live at the clubhouse, don't you?" I ask Chase.

"Yeah."

Thinking about him spending his nights at the bar picking up women is more unpleasant than I expected. It's not like I thought Chase had been a monk since we broke up, but it's another thing to know he's living there, in that rowdy scene. I've been to the *Savage Asylum* with him before and know how the girls throw themselves at the guys, sometimes even giving blowjobs or fucking them right there for everyone to see. I may have let Chase touch me in front of his brothers, but we never went that far, mostly because Chase didn't want anyone to see me that way.

Without a word, Chase turns off his truck and climbs out, so I do the same, following him up the porch steps and into the dark house. He flips on a few lights as we go.

"You can sleep in my old room if you want," he tells me.

Great, the one with the most memories.

Everything in the house is pretty much the same, just fewer family photos and knickknacks that I expect his parents took with them.

Chase's room up the stairs is neater and tidier than I remember.

"We have a housekeeper come and clean up every few weeks," he explains as if reading my mind. "Sheets should be clean. I hardly ever stay here. Just once in a while, to get away from the chaos."

I nod as I sit my duffle bag down on the floor.

"I'll, um, let you get changed," he says as he starts for the door. "If you need me, I'll be downstairs."

"Where were you when I needed you ten years ago?" I blurt out.

...

Chase

"*WHERE* WAS I?" I repeat in confusion as I reach up and shove my fingers through the front of my hair. "What the fuck, Sasha?"

"You were the first person I looked for when I woke up," she says. Her voice cracks when she continues, "And you weren't there. I thought you...I thought you were dead, because I couldn't imagine any other reason that you wouldn't be beside me."

"Are you fucking with me right now?" I ask. She has to be.

"Just answer the question!" she yells through her tears. "Where were you?"

"I was there!" I shout. "I was in the waiting room."

She shakes her head as tears stream down her face. "No, you weren't!"

"Yes, I was, goddamn it!" I exclaim as I stride up to her until our faces are only inches apart, so she can read the truth in my eyes. "I was waiting for days, worried to death about you, wanting to see you, to hold you, to tell you how fucking sorry I was, and you wouldn't let me!"

Choking on a sob, she says, "I wouldn't *let* you? I was barely able to open my eyes for the first few days!"

"You were awake enough to tell your parents that you never wanted to see me again and that you would never forgive me for hurting you," I remind her.

Sasha gasps and reels back like I slapped her. "What?"

"I'd caused you enough pain. I wasn't gonna stay around and keep making you upset. So, after three days, I finally left," I tell her.

"I was upset because you weren't there!" she shouts, bringing me up short.

"Then why didn't you call me and tell me you changed your mind?" I ask.

"Changed my mind?" she asks, then shoves both palms against my chest. "Changed my mind! I never changed my mind! Every fucking day I begged for you to come, and every day you broke my heart!"

"That's...I didn't know, sweetheart," I tell her as an invisible fist tightens around my neck, hearing her say that I broke her heart. "I thought when you said you never wanted to see me again that you meant fucking never..."

Sasha shakes her head emphatically back and forth. "I didn't say that."

"You did," I assure her. "When you first woke up. Maybe you don't remember because of the drugs..."

"*I. Didn't. Say. That,*" she repeats through clenched teeth. "I remember every moment from the time I woke up. The doctor telling me that I would need more surgeries, the nurses asking if I needed more pain medicine. And I remember telling them that all I wanted was to see you, to know if you were okay!"

"Are you sure? Everything was probably hazy," I tell her, knowing that she's mistaken.

"I remember my parents coming to see me in the recovery room," she goes on through the tears. "I asked them about you..."

"And?" I ask, needing her to keep going.

"They said that you walked away from the accident with a few scrapes and bruises."

"I fucking did," I grumble. "It's so goddamn unfair. I would've traded places with you in a heartbeat if I could've, sweetheart, I –"

"And they said that you...that you refused to come see me."

All the air is sucked out of my lungs like they've been attached to a fucking vacuum cleaner hose. With my next breath, I explode.

"That's fucking bullshit!" I shout so loud the neighbors a mile away probably heard it.

The weight of hearing all of this is almost too much for me to bear. Sasha's parents manipulated the two of us...and it cost us the past ten years.

My ass flops down on the bed as I force myself to go back to that hellish night, and into the next morning to make sure I'm not missing something.

"I waited," I tell Sasha. "I waited there at the hospital for you to change your mind. Every time your parents came out of your room, I asked them if you had. And each time they said no, that I should go home and give up. That you didn't need the stress."

"They wouldn't have lied to me," she says as she drops down on the bed next to me and stares into space, likely trying to convince herself, rather than convince me. "They wouldn't have hurt me like that. They knew how upset I was. I cried...I cried for weeks..."

Sasha's close to her parents, especially her father. But they've always been protective of her. They would've done *anything* to get me out of her life. So they took advantage of our shitty situation to split us up.

Reaching over for Sasha's right hand resting on her thigh, the one my name is on, I cover it with mine and give it a squeeze, relieved when she doesn't flinch or push me away.

"I'm sorry," I tell her softly, meaning for everything, but mostly because of our time apart caused by a stupid misunderstanding.

Sasha inhales a deep, shaky breath and then blows it out.

"Wow," she says, followed by a sniffle.

"I'll go get you some tissues," I tell her. But when I start to stand up, Sasha grabs my arm to pull me back down on the bed. One look at her face, and I know exactly what she wants, what she needs from me, because it's the same thing I need. We've waited too damn long for this moment, and I don't intend to waste another second.

Grabbing the side of her face, I cover her lips with mine, doing what I've dreamed of for so long that it's hard to believe it's actually happening. When Sasha moans and parts her lips for my tongue, I dive in and never look back. If this is a dream, I'm gonna make the fucking most out of it. My free hand clutches her side to pull her closer, and Sasha does me one better. She throws one of her long legs over my lap to straddle me, putting her in the perfect position for my hands to roam up her sexy shirt to get to her breasts.

"Fuck, they still fit my hands perfectly," I tell her as I give both a hard squeeze that makes Sasha gasp. Being the angel that she is, she rips the shirt over her head and tosses it to the floor to give my mouth full access.

"Oh my God," she gasps, arching her back and throwing her head back to push her tits toward me in offering. Her hands grasp my face between them while she grinds down onto my lap. Dragging her fingers through my facial hair, she says, "I love this fucking beard."

If my mouth weren't full of her nipple, I would respond. As it is, I'm not willing to stop sucking on her just yet.

Sasha's not content with just a lap dance. She pushes my cut down my arms and then lifts my white tee up, forcing me to remove my mouth from her breasts as it comes over my head. When she reaches for my pants and pops the button, I know she's tired of foreplay already, even though I just got started and want to cover every inch of her body with my mouth. But it's been too long since I've been inside of her, so I start undoing her pants too. Neither of us gets very far since we're both sitting, so I pick her up and lie her on her back in the middle of the bed to get us naked.

CHAPTER FOURTEEN

Sasha

CHASE LOOKS DOWN AT ME WITH A MIXTURE OF AWE AND NEED on his face as he stands next to the bed and undresses. His capable hands have his boots, socks, and pants off in record-breaking time while I take in his tall, massive frame, covered in muscles and tattoos. Some are old, like my name in faded black cursive ink on his chest, but there are other new ones on his chest that I can't wait to examine closer. He's bigger than he was when we were together, and I'm pretty sure I had forgotten how long and thick his cock was, more substantial than any of the few lovers I was with after him.

He watches me the entire time as he crawls across the bed and then kneels over my legs. Leaning forward, his mouth kisses a path down the center of my chest to my belly button while his hands start tugging my tight pants and panties down my thighs.

"Chase," I moan as my eyes close, and I throw my head back. His thick beard feels so soft moving down my stomach that my hips roll to try and press into it a little more. Like he knows what I want, he runs his lips up and down my stomach a few more times, making sure his beard brushes my skin along the way.

I'm halfway to coming just from the glide of his beard before I realize he's finally worked my pants all the way down my legs. I notice this when his mouth moves away from my body, causing my eyes to blink open.

Chase kneels over me, my pants and panties paused at my ankles when his gaze locks on my scarred knee.

Sitting up, I finish removing my bottoms and then tug on his beard, telling him, "Get back up here."

His head falls forward as he curses. "I'm sorry, sweetheart. So fucking sorry," he tells me while his head is still bowed.

"It wasn't your fault," I assure him as I comb my fingers through the top of his hair, meaning the accident and now...everything that followed because of my parents. "I never blamed you for the accident, Chase."

He shakes his head but doesn't look at me. "I wasn't paying attention. I should've seen him coming..."

"Our light was green. I remember," I say to him. "The guy was drunk and didn't stop for his red light."

"I made him pay for what he did," he says softly.

"I know," I reply. "He made a mistake, one that hurt us both for a long time. I blamed *him* for everything..." I trail off. "Before that moment, my life was perfect. And then it felt like it ended."

"Mine too," Chase agrees. "Every night I prayed I'd go to sleep and wake up to find out it was all just a fucking nightmare. Then, each morning I woke up, and it all stayed the same – I'd lost you."

"We're here now," I tell him, tugging on his beard hard enough that he has to look up at me. His eyes are shimmering and filled with so much pain I can't bear another second. "I kept waiting for you, Chase. Please don't make me wait any longer."

That was apparently the right thing to say to put him into motion. He leans forward and presses a trail of kisses up my scar before moving to my inner thigh and then swiping his tongue through my slit. "I'm gonna eat this pussy like a starving man later," he promises as he moves up my body. "But right now, I have to be inside of you."

"Yes," I agree, reaching for his face to pull it down to mine.

Both of us pour ten years into our kiss. It's so rough and brutal that our teeth clash and tongues get bitten, but it's exactly what I need. Chase slips a finger inside of me and then two, pumping them in and out of me with the same ferocity as our kiss, making me come so hard my entire body levitates off the mattress.

Chase's much bigger, heavier body presses me back down when his hips thrust forward, and he enters me. He's so big that it takes a while for him to work himself all the way in from this angle. His mouth swallows my moans as my body stretches to take every inch of him until I'm full, and he finally possesses me the way only Chase has ever been able to do.

"Let me love you the way you deserve this time," he says as he looks down at me with his arms holding his weight off of me while he's buried deep. "Then I'm gonna fuck your brains out the way you love."

Slipping my hands down to grab his clenched ass cheeks, I tell him, "I'll take anything I can get."

Dipping his head to kiss my cheek, Chase's beard tickles the side of my face, and he whispers, "Don't forget you said that tomorrow when your pussy aches so bad you won't be able to take anything but my tongue." His lips move down to my neck, kissing me at the spot that makes my belly clench. "I promise I'll keep licking it until it's all better," he assures me.

"I can't wait to ride your beard," I tell him with a smile as I run my fingers through it.

"Fuck yes," he says before he captures my lips again and finally begins to move inside of me.

...

Chase

"Making love" was never my and Sasha's style as kids, but I don't mind it now that I've learned a little patience in the bedroom.

But I can't deny that fucking Sasha is still by far the single best thing I've ever experienced in my life.

That's why I don't give her any time to recover after our first time before I slide down her body and flick my tongue over her clit, making her hips bounce on the mattress.

"Are you on birth control?" I ask her between flicks.

"A little late...for that question...now. *Oh God*!" she cries out, and her thighs fall open, an invitation for me to do whatever I want to her.

"Sasha?" I say, removing my tongue and waiting for her to answer me.

"Yes," she replies before her fingers tug on my hair to push my mouth back down on her.

I give her a few licks before asking, "How many men have you been with?"

"Really?" she huffs.

"Answer, and I'll keep going."

"Ugh," she groans. "Fine, three."

"Three," I repeat, glad that I don't know their names so I won't go punch them in their dicks for entering *my* pussy.

"What about you?" Sasha asks as she raises up on her elbows. "Can you even count that high?"

"Can I count to ten? Yeah, I can," I reply.

"Bullshit!" she exclaims.

"I've been inside ten other pussies," I clarify. "A few different mouths. That's it."

"One a year? You expect me to believe that?" Sasha asks.

"It's the truth, sweetheart. I knew a million pussies couldn't replace yours, so I didn't try to burn through them all."

Her head falls back on the bed, and then she says, "I hate my parents."

"Stop thinking about your parents while I'm licking your pussy," I warn her. "We'll deal with them later, yeah?"

"Deal with them?" she repeats. "How do I deal with them after they destroyed what we had, knowing I was miserable without you?"

"They didn't destroy what we had," I tell her as I crawl up her body to hover over her. "We can pick right back up from where we left off. It'll be like we took a little break."

"A little break that lasted a fucking decade," Sasha adds. "And we're different now. I don't know if we can pick right back up."

"Yes, we fucking can," I assure her, because I can't lose her again.

"Chase," she starts, but I put a finger to her lips to hush her.

"We're not deciding anything right now. Let's just enjoy our first night together in way too long and go one day at a time."

Sasha opens her mouth and bites my finger gently before sucking on it, making my dick hard as a goddamn rock again.

"How do you want me to take you this time?" I ask her as I cup her breast in my hand and lean down to kiss her nipple.

"Doggie," she replies as she squirms under my mouth.

Releasing her nipple with an audible pop, I tell her, "Great fucking answer. Roll over."

Lifting her head to give me a quick kiss, she says, "I missed you and your bossy ways in the bedroom."

"I missed everything about you, sweetheart," I tell her honestly. "Now let me see that ass I missed in the air, ready and waiting for me."

Grinning, she rolls over. I slap her sexy ass cheek just because I can. It's mine for tonight, hopefully, longer. And then I slam inside, claiming her, owning her while she cries out with each hard thrust. Remembering how she always liked it a little rough, I grab a handful of her long hair, making Sasha moan when I give it a tug to force her head backward to bring my mouth to hers. I kiss the fuck out of her too, because there are not enough words in the English language for me to tell her how goddamn happy I am to have her back in my life and my bed again, because she never left my heart or my soul.

CHAPTER FIFTEEN

Sasha

AFTER OUR THIRD INCREDIBLE ROUND OF MIND-BLOWING SEX, I clean up in the bathroom, too exhausted to shower, and then throw back the sheets to get back in bed naked with Chase in his childhood room.

"Get in here," he grumbles, sounding as tired as I am. He holds out his arm for me to snuggle up against his side.

Despite the fact that I can barely hold my eyes open any longer, there's a ridiculously sappy smile stretched across my face; and it doesn't seem to be disappearing anytime soon. Not that I want it to.

Chase makes me happy. I'd forgotten how much of a joy it was to simply be in his presence. Sure, he can be violent when necessary, and he's a little rough and dirty; but with everything he says and does, he makes me feel like I'm the center of his universe. I know who he is deep down. While on the outside he's an outlaw biker who can easily pull a trigger to end someone's life, inside he's still a big softie when it comes to me. I wouldn't change a single thing about him even if I could, because the danger that surrounds him and the

MC is one of the reasons I was attracted to him in the first place. Life with Chase would never be boring. It would be thrilling and exciting, a roller coaster with incredible highs and lows that remind you to never take anything for granted.

Chase pulls me closer to him until my head is resting on his chest, right above my name. I press my lips to his still damp skin and let my fingertips roam up and down his chest and abs, unable to get enough of him.

It's too bad that my parents took something so great out of my life for so long. I love them dearly, but knowing that they intentionally lied to both of us to keep us apart is infuriating. I didn't think I would ever get this feeling back or even ever want Chase back.

Now I know that he was hurting as much as I was after the wreck, if not more so because he was blaming himself.

"The house is listed under a dummy corp," Chase says, and I wonder why he's telling me this now. "It doesn't have any ties directly to me, my parents, or the MC, and no one followed us," his voice trails off in explanation. "They won't find us here."

"Even if they did, I know I would be safe with you," I tell him with another kiss to his chest.

"Hell yeah you would," he agrees. "Unless they bring an army..."

"There's no army coming. Get some rest," I tell him.

"Don't you fucking disappear when I wake up," he orders in a mumble.

"I'm staying right here," I assure him before I finally let my eyes drift closed.

...

Chase

Sasha's still in my arms, asleep on my chest when I wake up to the sound of my phone ringing from inside my pants pocket across the room.

I'm surprised I didn't squeeze her to death like a boa constrictor in my sleep. The first few times I drifted off, I startled awake having nightmares about the accident, thinking that last night was just a dream.

It was real. I know because the goddamn phone keeps ringing until I have a headache and Sasha rolls over and covers her head with her pillow, making me crack a smile.

Figuring it must be important if they're that damn persistent, and since only my brothers and parents have my number, I finally force myself to leave the warm heaven that is my childhood bed and walk naked over to the pile of clothing in the floor. The phone is ringing again as I pull it out of my jean pocket, Torin's name lit up on the screen.

"What?" I answer as I walk out in the hallway so that I won't bother Sasha.

"Where the hell are you?" Torin growls.

"Why?" I ask rather than tell him my location. He wants to keep shit from me; well, I can do the same.

"Get your ass back to the clubhouse now!" he orders before hanging up on me.

Fuck.

It'd be easy to say to hell with him and crawl back in the bed with Sasha, if he was just my brother. But he's also our MC president, and I'm pretty sure it was *that* version of him calling. If I start blowing him off, it looks bad for the club, so I'll cave and go.

Grabbing a quick shower and changing into some of my old jeans and tee in my bedroom, I sit down to tie my boots up. Once my cut is back on, I'm ready to go.

There's no way I'm leaving Sasha here by herself, though, so I step into the hallway to call Abe.

"What the fuck man?" he grumbles when he eventually answers. "Do you know what fucking time it is?"

"Time for you to get up and do me a favor," I reply with a grin.

He curses and mumbles some unintelligible shit before he finally asks, "What do you want?"

"Can you come out to the farmhouse? Sasha's here, and Hector Cruz is after her, trying to get to me."

"Fuck," he replies.

"Yeah. And Torin wants me at the clubhouse. Are you there?"

"Yep, and I think I just heard him shouting at someone right before you called."

"That was probably me," I say. "Anyway. Get here as soon as you can."

"Let me take a piss, and I'm on my way."

"Thanks, Abe," I tell him.

While I wait, I call to check in with the prospects. Holden doesn't answer, so I try Maddox.

"Yo, Chase, man. Torin is on the rampage. He told us to get back to the clubhouse, so we're about to walk in."

"Okay," I reply. "I'm on my way too, so I'll take the heat off of you."

"Appreciate it," Maddox replies.

"Any problems last night?" I ask.

"Nope."

"Good," I say before I hang up.

Back in the bedroom, the sheets have come down to Sasha's waist, revealing her long blonde hair trailing down her bare back and just a hint of her tit since she's lying on her stomach with the pillow still on her head. Covering her back up, I squat down, eye level with her face and lift the pillow to kiss her on the neck, just below her ear. That has her squirming and moaning instantly, like I knew it would. And while I don't have time to take care of her right now, you can bet your ass I will as soon as I get back. In the meantime, I want to leave her with the reminder of last night and all the good things to come later.

"Mornin', sweetheart," I tell her softly as she starts to blink her eyes open. I brush the hair from out of her face so she can see.

"Why are you up...and...have you had a shower?" she asks. "What time is it?"

"Early. Go back to sleep. I've got to go to the clubhouse, but Abe's on his way here to stay with you."

"Okay," she agrees, rather than argue that she doesn't need a babysitter. Shit is too risky right now. And while I can't figure out any way that they would find us here, I'm not taking any chances.

"I'll be back soon and make you breakfast," I promise.

"Good," Sasha says.

When I hear Abe's bike rumbling down the road, I give her a quick kiss on the lips and then head down the steps to the front door to let him in.

Killing the engine, Abe says, "You look like you had a better night than me."

"What happened?" I ask, noticing his face is bruised and cut up.

"Couple of Aces assholes came into *Avalon* and started messing with the girls. Took a few of us to help Cooper and Miles get 'em out, but not without it coming to blows."

"Jesus," I mutter. "What the hell were those assholes thinking?" I ask. They're brazen as fuck selling their crank on our streets, but blatantly coming into one of the businesses they know is owned by the Savage Kings is suicidal.

"Don't know," Abe replies. "A few of them caused a fight over at the *Iron Carousel* too. Dalton and Reece handled it without needing backup."

"They're getting too fucking brave," I tell him. "And I think Hector Cruz is behind their confidence. If he's backing them, they think they're untouchable."

"Shit's getting fucked sideways," Abe agrees with a shake of his head. "So, what's with the reporter?"

"We're back together," I tell him. "Keep your eyes and hands off of her."

He holds his palm up in the air in surrender. "You know I wouldn't try and fuck with your girl. I've seen your ink. I get it, brother."

"Good," I tell him. "Call me if you need me. I should be back soon."

"Got it," he agrees before he goes inside, and I climb in my truck.

Abe is one of the few guys I would trust alone with Sasha. I know she'll be in good hands with him.

The *Savage Asylum* is still closed this early, so I unlock the doors, punch in my security code to the clubhouse, and jog down the stairs to find Torin.

"What the hell have you done?" he barks from his seat at the table at me when I step into the room. The two prospects are standing there like scolded children since they haven't earned the right to sit in one of our chairs yet.

"Well, let's see," I say as I walk around to take my seat on Torin's right. Leaning back, I stroke my hand over my beard and tell him from the beginning. "I wrestled with an asshole Trooper in his pool, and he didn't wake up. He was working for Hector, by the way. Also, he was planning to kidnap Sasha to get to me, so he could kill me," I explain. "Then, when I got to Sasha's house the next night, there were two fuckers watching her, so I lured them into the house and took them out before they could put a bullet in me."

"Three more dead bodies means Hector is gonna come at us with everything he has!" Torin roars. His face is blood red, and I'm pretty sure he wants to throttle me right fucking here.

"Let's not fucking forget how this all started," I remind him.

"By you losing your fucking temper and killing one of his guys and hurting two others on the highway!" my brother bellows.

"Do you really want them to hear this?" I ask, pointing over at the prospects.

"Get out!" Torin yells at them, and they leave, closing the door behind them.

"You're making shit worse, Chase. You can't keep going around killing everyone you think deserves it," Torin starts, his jaw clenching between every sentence. "This woman is making you lose your shit and jeopardize this club."

"That woman is the best thing that's ever happened to me. I lost her for ten years, and now I'll do whatever it takes to keep her safe, just like you would do for Kennedy."

"Exactly!" Torin exclaims.

"What does that mean?" I ask through narrowed eyes. "What does this shit with Hector have to do with Kennedy?"

"Goddamn it," he mutters before he gets to his feet to pace. The more he does that, the more I worry that things truly are out of control, and he just won't admit it. Usually, Torin is calm, cool-headed. Now, he's starting to look fucking frazzled. "Hector's got me by the fucking balls, okay? And every time I start to think I'm gonna be free of him, he squeezes even tighter."

"Fuck, Torin. What's he got on you?"

"He's blackmailing me," he answers, making my fist clench with the urge to smash them into the fucker's face.

"With what?" I ask.

Torin shakes his head, refusing to answer.

"Bro, you know I can't help you if I don't know what's going on."

"It's something that would ruin me. That's all you need to know," he replies as he scrubs his hands over his face and starts pacing again.

"So, Hector is fucking you over, and he wants me dead. There's a simple solution to this problem..."

"Fuck, I wish it was that easy," Torin says with a heavy sigh as he looks at the ceiling. "He warned me that if he dies, there's someone else who has the tape and will release it."

"What fucking tape?" I ask.

"One that will take everything from me," Torin answers.

"It can't be that bad," I tell him. I know my brother; he doesn't put a toe across the line unless he absolutely has to. Whatever he did can't be that damn bad.

"Look, let me handle this, okay?" Torin asks. "I make the decisions, and you follow them. You hate any fucking responsibility, which is why you refused to take the gavel, so leave the important shit to me."

"You're right. I've never had any interest in leading. That's all on you. But you're hiding shit from everyone. All those plates you're spinning are gonna come crashing down on your head real soon. I think the pressure is getting to you and you're scared to do what needs to be done."

"Just give me a few days," Torin says. "If I have to kill Hector, then I will. But I'm trying to figure a way out of this without spilling any more blood. Don't you think you've done enough of that?"

"I did what was necessary to keep Sasha safe and keep me alive. I won't apologize for it," I tell him. "Now, I still have to watch my back and Sasha's. I can't do that shit forever. You keep waiting around, doing nothing, and you're gonna get me killed. Eventually, Hector will get the drop on me and put a bullet in my head. When he does, that's on you," I tell Torin before I get up from the table and walk out.

Torin doesn't think I ever take responsibility for shit. Well, I'm disappointed that my brother, our leader, doesn't have the balls to man up and take responsibility for whatever he did to start this war.

He can blame me for being a hot-head who escalated things on the highway; but when someone makes threats, I don't sit around and wait to see if they'll go through with them or not. That's a good way to end up dead.

CHAPTER SIXTEEN

Sasha

I lie in Chase's bed, staring at the ceiling and just soaking up all the details from last night. I miss him, but I love how at least the bed still smells like his soap or aftershave mixed with leather. It's masculine and alluring, making me want to drown in the scent.

Just the word *drown* makes me feel guilty, thinking about Travis, the highway patrolman. I knew something was off with him that night at *Darren's*. There was a bad vibe coming off of him. That's why I told him I didn't feel well and got up to leave before our meal even arrived. He scared me.

Deep down, despite his badge and clean-cut appearance, I knew he wasn't a good guy. While I hate what Chase did to him, I know he only did it to protect me. Chase would do *anything* to keep me safe, which is why he must have felt so awful after the accident. There was nothing Chase could've done to avoid the truck crashing into us.

At the time, I kept asking myself what if we had stayed in the tattoo shop's parking lot for just another few seconds. What if I had kissed Chase one last time or took a minute to tell him how much he meant to me...could we have avoided the accident?

But that's not how life works. There's no way for us to predict the future, which is why we were riding through that exact intersection at that exact point in time.

The truck was meant to hit us, just like my path was meant to cross with Chase's again because of another collision. Despite us going our different ways — me to college and into a career in television and Chase moving up in the MC — fate took us both on a path back to each other. This is where we're meant to be.

Even though my parents wanted to keep us apart...

After I take a quick shower and dry my hair, I put on one of Chase's black Savage King's shirts and then sit down on the bed with my phone, ready to get answers from them.

As soon as I hear my father's voice, so loving as he greets me like every other time while keeping his lie from me, I ask him, "How could you?"

"What's that, sweetie?" he replies.

"You know what! You and mom have lied to me for ten years!" I say as my throat begins to burn from trying to hold back the tears and emotion.

"Calm down. What are you yelling about, Sash?" he says.

"Chase," I tell him.

"Who...are you kidding? Chase Fury? Why are you bringing up that loser –"

"I loved him!" I interrupt when he tries to badmouth him, as he did so often those first few weeks. "I loved him, and you pushed us apart. How could you tell him that I would never forgive him, knowing how much it would hurt him and me both?" I ask. "Now I don't know how I can forgive you and Mom."

"We did you a favor, Sasha! He would've dragged you down, knocked you up or worse! Without him holding you back, you went to college; you have the career you've always wanted..."

"I wanted him more," I reply before I end the call, too angry to keep speaking to that man right now.

My parents have been there for me through everything. They saw my tears, the sadness that crushed me, the depression of losing so much and not understanding why. I couldn't believe that Chase would abandon me; that was the hardest part to cope with. And now I know why I questioned that so much, because in my heart I knew that he wouldn't do that to me.

"Everything okay up there?" a gruff voice asks from downstairs, reminding me that I'm not alone.

"Yeah, sorry," I call back to him. Tossing the phone on the bed, I swipe my fingers under each of my eyes to wipe away the moisture, and then look for a pair of Chase's shorts to throw on. "Just a second and I'll be right down," I say as I pull the red athletic shorts up my legs and then roll the elastic waistband over a few times to make them stay on.

Finally decent, I jog down the stairs and come face to face with a big guy with black hair and a beard even longer than Chase's. Wearing the MC's black leather cut over a black wife beater to reveal the sleeve of dark tattoos covering his right arm, he looks strong enough to tear the head off of a man with his bare hands.

The fact that Chase trusted him to stay here alone with me must mean that he trusts him more than anyone else.

"Hi. I'm Sasha," I tell him with a smile as I hold out my right hand to him.

"The mysterious Sasha behind his ink," he says as he shakes my hand in his large, calloused paw. "You know, I made the mistake of asking Chase about that tat the first day we roomed together in prison. I thought it would be an icebreaker, you know, get him talking about his old lady or daughter, someone he cared about to soften him up since he looked like he wanted to punch me. Turned out, that question was the detonator on his hair-trigger. He socked me right in the jaw," he says with a chuckle as he releases my hand to rub the left side of his face. "We've been tight ever since."

"Wow," I reply in surprise to all of that information.

"I'm Abe, by the way," he says.

"So, I'm guessing you guys met about six or seven years ago when he was in for aggravated assault?" I ask.

"That would be it," Abe agrees. "I was in for grand theft auto. Real life is not like the video game at all. If you try to run over a cop, they put out the spike strip and then drag your ass right to prison."

"Good to know," I tell him. "What kind of car was it?" I ask curiously.

Smiling wide, he says, "A black 1957 Jaguar XKSS."

"Nice," I reply. "You've got great taste. Those are rare and worth a fortune. Only, what, fifteen or sixteen ever made?"

Abe arches one of his black eyebrows in surprise and says, "No wonder Chase laid claim to you on his skin. Beautiful woman who know cars. Well, that's a hard combo to find."

"Why, thank you," I reply. "And I'm pretty sure Chase loved my car before he loved me – a cherry red 1967 Mustang convertible."

"No shit," Abe says.

"My dad and I rebuilt it together," I say, hating that all of my good memories of my parents are now tainted with their lies. "It took us two years to put it back together. And then a few weeks before my eighteenth birthday, my dad gave me the keys and told me it had always been mine."

"Nice," Abe says. "You still have it?"

"I do," I reply. Narrowing my eyes, I point my finger at him and tell him, "Don't even think about trying to steal it."

He holds up his palms with a deep chuckle. "My grand theft days are over, doll."

"That's probably for the best," I tell him. "Prison doesn't seem like much fun."

"It's not," he agrees. "But I'm glad I met Chase. He talked me and my younger brother Gabe into prospecting with the club when I was released a month after him. Best decision I ever made."

"It's nice when something good comes from something shitty," I tell him.

"Speaking of good things, you got any cute friends, preferably redheads that you could hook me up with?"

"Hmm, maybe" I look him over slowly from head to toe. My roommate from college is a natural redhead, and I think she should be back in the Carolinas soon after a year hiatus. "But I don't think I know you well enough to date my friend just yet. I'll have to keep an eye on you and see if you can earn it."

Grinning, Abe gives me a nod. "Fair enough."

"So, tell me about Chase the last few years," I say as I lead the way into the living room to take a seat on the old sofa.

"He's been a hotheaded, grumpy, overall pain in the fucking ass, pretty much," Abe informs me as he sits in one of the armchairs across from me.

"So, not much has changed, huh?" I ask.

"Guess not," Abe agrees with a chuckle.

CHAPTER SEVENTEEN

Chase

If Torin knew that I was on my way to his house, he would kick my ass.

But I need to find out more about how deep he is with Hector, and Kennedy may be able to help with that.

I would never throw my brother under the bus with her. I just need to ask a few questions.

Before I change my mind, I walk up the steps to the side door of their enormous beach house and ring the doorbell. Kennedy answers right away.

"Chase," she says, her warm, brown eyes widening in surprise. "Is everything okay?"

"Yeah, yeah, of course," I tell her. I should've realized that showing up without calling would worry her. Actually, I don't think Torin has invited me over since I helped them move in right after their wedding. "Have you got a second?" I ask.

"Sure, come in," she says, opening the door wider. "I was just putting away some of the baby's clothes."

"How's the little man doin'?" I ask as I follow her into the living room where there's a bucket of laundry.

"He's raising hell in here," she replies with a grin as she sits down and then pulls out a tiny blue outfit to fold it. "I think he's ready to bust out too."

"Looks like he's getting big," I say, and Kennedy shoots me a glare. "Not you. I didn't say you're getting big. I said he was. You know, your belly."

"Uh-huh," she replies with a good-natured roll of her eyes before she goes back to folding. "So what's up? You must be here to talk to me since you know Torin's always at the clubhouse."

"Right," I agree. Reaching up to smooth out my beard to figure how to approach the subject, I decide to start with, "Do you think Torin's been acting a little...off?"

"Off?" Kennedy repeats. Tilting her head to the side to consider it, she says, "I dunno. I mean, he's been pretty freaked out ever since I told him I was pregnant. I know he's happy; it was all just unexpected. I figured he was worried about being a father..."

"How about more recently?" I ask.

"Hmm," she says. "I mean, he's a little stressed out about the MC expansion."

"The expansion?" I repeat in confusion.

"Yeah, you know, for the new bar or whatever."

"Sure," I reply, even though I know for a fact there isn't any talk about expanding for a bar or anything else. I may screw off most of the time, but I'm at the table for every damn meeting.

"Has Torin used any of you guys' money for it?" I ask.

"Well, yeah," she answers as if that's obvious.

"How much?"

"I think it was about six hundred thousand recently, more a few months ago. Torin pretty much cleared out our savings, but there's enough coming in from the other investments that it's not a big deal," she says. "Besides, he said that the MC would pay him back."

"Yeah," I agree rather than call my brother out on yet another lie.

I get that he doesn't want Kennedy to know about the blackmail, but that's a fuck-ton of money going to some asshole for a tape that Torin doesn't want anyone to see.

"Is everything okay, Chase? All these questions...you're starting to worry me," Kennedy says with her hands resting on her bump.

"No, it's fine, sweetheart," I tell her, so she will hopefully let it go. "I just wanted to check in with you about Torin to make sure he's okay. He doesn't talk to me much lately, and he'd be pissed if he knew I came by bothering you."

"You're not bothering me," she says with a broad smile. "It's good having you stop by. How's everything been going?"

"Great," I reply honestly. "Sasha and I are back together, or at least getting there."

"Really! Oh, wow, that's great, Chase," Kennedy says excitedly. "I'm so happy for you even though I don't really know what happened to you guys. She must have been important to you since you have the ink."

"She was. She is," I correct. Standing up, I say, "And I should get back to her."

"Well, yeah," she agrees. It takes Kennedy a moment to push herself off the sofa; but when she does, she comes over and hugs me. "I want to meet her," she says when she pulls away.

"Okay, sure," I tell her, thinking that's a great idea. "I may bring her to the clubhouse soon and would love it if you were there too. She probably won't like the other women."

"Oh, you mean the clubs sluts you've slept with?" Kennedy teases.

"Yeah, those women," I agree. "They're gonna be jealous, but I think Sasha can handle herself. She didn't have a problem with them before when we were together."

"She'll step up and put those girls in their place if she intends to stick around," Kennedy replies. "That's what I had to do to make sure they got the message that Torin was taken and not to go near him or I'd claw their eyeballs out."

Chuckling, I tell her, "Yeah, Sasha's probably gonna need some pointers from you."

"Anytime," she agrees. "Bye, Chase."

"Bye, Kennedy," I say.

On the way out, I can't help but think that Torin is a lucky son of a bitch to have someone like his old lady. I just hope he doesn't fuck it up by keeping whatever the hell he's done a secret.

CHAPTER EIGHTEEN

Sasha

As soon as I hear the gravel crunching under the weight of tires, I jump up from the sofa and rush over to look out the window.

"Calm your tits, girly. Let me see who it is first," Abe says, making me laugh when he jumps in front of me, blocking my view. "Okay. It's just Chase."

"I knew that," I tell him with a smile.

Unable to wait another second to see him, I rush out the front door and down the porch steps barefooted. I meet Chase in front of his truck as he comes around it, jumping into his arms, wrapping my arms around his neck and legs around his waist to kiss him.

I realize Chase is holding a plastic grocery bag in one of his hands when they both come around on my ass to hold me up while his tongue invades my mouth, making my lower body ignite with need.

"I missed you too," he says against my lips as he carries me into the house. Chuckling, he adds, "And I probably just broke all the eggs I was gonna make you for breakfast."

"You can buy more later," I tell him with a nip to his bottom lip. "All I want right now is you naked and inside of me."

"Your pussy's not too sore from last night?" he asks.

"A little, but I can think of a few other places on my body for you to put your cock," I tell him.

"Fuck, yes," he agrees before he attacks my mouth again.

"And I'll take that as my cue to take off," Abe says as he passes by us on the porch steps.

Neither Chase nor I even pause a second in our kiss to tell him goodbye, not until his bike revs up. Glancing over, I watch him kick up dust and a few rocks as he drives off.

"Where's your bike?" I ask Chase when he carries me the rest of the way inside the house.

"At the clubhouse," he answers.

"I want you to take me for a ride," I tell him.

"You can go for a ride on this cock," he replies as he squeezes my ass to grind me down over the bulge behind his zipper.

"I wanna ride both," I tell him as I kiss my way up his neck and we go to the kitchen. "Maybe at the same time again." Whispering in his ear, I ask, "Do you remember how good it was that night we fucked on your bike?"

"God, yes," he groans. "How could I forget? It was the last time I was inside of you before last night. I came so hard..."

He tosses his grocery bag on the counter and then starts to set me down on the kitchen table.

"Put me on my knees," I tell him.

"No," he says, drawing me up short. Before I can ask why not, he reaches for the sides of his shirt that I'm wearing and pulls it over my head. "First, I'm gonna eat your pussy."

"Why can't we do both?" I ask as I unzip his jeans. Chase still doesn't wear underwear, so once the denim falls to his knees, his long, hard dick bobs free.

Shoving the shorts I'm wearing down my legs, I scoot back just a little on the table and turn around to hang my head off the edge. I fist Chase's length to bring the blunt tip to my mouth.

"God, I've missed your lips stretched around my cock," he says, letting me suck him a few times before he leans over and spreads my raised knees apart to lean over and bury his head between them. His beard tickles my stomach and his tongue circling my clit feels so damn good that it takes me a minute to recover before I can take him deep into my throat again.

As soon as Chase adds a finger inside of me, I start coming. But I no longer have to worry about sucking him because his hips pump in and out of my mouth the way he needs. It's a little rough, and I almost gag a few times, but I still love it, making him lose control. I hate knowing that other women have been taking care of his needs because I wasn't there to do it. I want to show him that I can make him feel even better than they can.

"God, that's good, sweetheart. I'm so...fucking...close," he tells me through panting breaths before he thrusts deep one last time and fills my mouth with his hot release. "Fuck, I can't stand up," he grumbles as he drops to his knees on the kitchen floor.

I start to roll over and get up when Chase jerks on my hair to pull my mouth down so he can cover it with an upside-down kiss. When he pulls away, he says, "I'm a fucking asshole."

"What?" I ask, finally rolling over to get up on my hands and knees, so I don't have to keep looking at his face upside down.

"I had the girls at the club suck my dick while you were on the news."

He did what now?

When I realize what he's saying, I bite down on my lip to keep from smiling.

"That's...sort of sweet, I guess," I tell him.

"It's fucked up is what it is," he says as he pulls himself up using the edge of the table and then fixes his jeans.

"A little bit," I tell him. "I thought of you whenever I was with someone else," I admit.

"I don't want to hear about you and other men," he says, scrubbing a hand down his face and shaking his head.

"They weren't very good," I assure him. "Or as big as you."

Giving me a small grin, he says, "Well, I guess that's okay then."

"You're the only man who's made me come while we're fucking," I add. "Probably because I made them all use condoms, which desensitizes everything."

"I fucking always use condoms," Chase informs me. "You're the only woman I ever trusted not to lie to try and get knocked up."

"That would be a shitty thing to do," I agree as I swing my legs around and climb down off the dinner table. Chase's parents would be scandalized if they knew we went down on each other where they had family dinners.

"The club girls are desperate to be someone's old lady," he says. "I wouldn't put it past one of them."

"Are the other guys as careful as you?" I ask.

"No. And they're idiots," he replies with a chuckle. "Now how about I see if there are any eggs still in one piece and make you breakfast."

"Sounds perfect," I tell him, wrapping my arms around his neck to kiss him. "Thanks for not knocking anyone up while we were apart."

"Thanks for not getting knocked up while we were apart," he tells me, then slaps my bare ass. "Put some clothes on and quit distracting me before we both starve to death."

Laughing, I walk over and pick up the black Savage Kings tee and put it on again with nothing else.

"The bearded skull looks sexy as hell on you," Chase says when he looks over and sees me dressed again. "You were made to wear it."

"Do any of the other guys have old ladies?" I ask.

Getting out the pans he needs from the cabinet, Chase says,

"Torin's married. I think I mentioned that the other day. Kennedy is expecting their son any time now."

"You're gonna be an uncle!" I exclaim. "That's so exciting."

"Yeah, I can't wait to meet him. Kennedy's huge, so it shouldn't be much longer."

"Good for them," I say.

"Then there's War. He has a former old lady who's fucking insane, so he has sole custody of his three-year-old son."

"Wow," I mutter. "I bet it's not easy being in the MC and having kids."

"This shit the last few days is not the way we normally do things," he says, reaching into the grocery bag to pull out the eggs, a pack of sausage and a can of biscuits. "Usually it's pretty calm. All I know is that things are probably gonna get worse before they get better."

"Was the highway guy the first one you...you know?" I ask.

"First man I killed? Yeah," he answers. "After that, shit just started snowballing out of control with Hector."

"Yeah," I agree. "The last few days have been big news days. Speaking of which, I need to go to work this afternoon."

"Call in sick, sweetheart. At least through the weekend," Chase says, turning away from the kitchen counter to cross his arms over his chest. "Torin asked me to give him a little time to figure this fucking mess out. If that doesn't work, I'll take care of Hector myself. Then it's back to normal."

"Right, back to normal after you kill the bad guy," I say like it's that simple.

"Please take some time off," he asks again, even pulling out a please. "I need to keep you here, with me."

"And how do you plan to convince me to stay?" I ask with a grin.

"I have my ways," he replies before he turns around and gets back to work, knowing I'll cave.

"Can we go to the clubhouse and then take your bike out?" I ask.

"Yeah, I can take you to the clubhouse," he agrees. I wait for him to mention the bike, but he doesn't say anything further about it, just like he dodged my question about taking me for a ride earlier.

I get the feeling that Chase is still thinking about the wreck that happened years ago and is worried about having me on the back of his bike again.

Hopefully, I'll be able to convince him to change his mind.

CHAPTER NINETEEN

Chase

After breakfast, Sasha and I went back to bed, but not to get any sleep.

Everything was going great too, until I took another quick shower. I walked back into the bedroom just as Sasha was ending a phone call with someone. When I asked who she was talking to, she simply told me it was work stuff.

I didn't push her because things are so fucking good between us. But it's been an hour, and Sasha's barely said a few words to me. Something's on her mind; I just don't know what.

"You okay?" I ask her as I cut the engine on my truck in the *Savage Asylum* parking lot.

"Yeah," she answers. Glancing over at the neon sign on the building, she says, "Guess I'm a little nervous about going in and seeing the women who took my place."

"No one could ever take your place, sweetheart," I tell her honestly. Reaching over the console, I grab her hand and bring it up to my lips to kiss her knuckles. The gesture may not seem like much to her, but in the MC, the only hand a King kisses is his queen's – his old lady's. It's how the other brothers know that a woman's been claimed by a member to make sure they show them some respect, unlike the club sluts who get shared like public domain.

"Come on," I say, letting her hand go so we can get out. Before we walk through the door, I grab Sasha's hand again, intertwining our fingers, then step into the bar.

No shit, the whole place goes silent, other than the jukebox playing a rock song through the speakers. Every head turns in our direction; jaws are gaping, eyes are about to bulge out of their sockets. It's the damndest thing I've ever seen.

"Everyone meet Sasha. Sasha, meet everyone," I say since we seem to have the floor.

"Hi!" she says with a grin and a wave. Wearing her leather pants and sexy shirt again, it's easy to see why she has every man's eye in the room. The jealousy wafting off the women is so thick I nearly choke on it.

I lead her up to the bar, hoping the onlookers will fucking get on with it already and stop staring.

"What can I get you?" Turtle asks. He's an older fellow, my dad's age and balding. While he's never been patched in as a member, he's been a hang-around for twenty years now. He helps Fast Eddie, our oldest member, with his salvage yard business and towing company, which means the Kings keep them busy. A few nights a week Turtle also bartends for the hell of it.

"Beer?" I ask Sasha.

"Sure," she agrees. "Bud Light."

"Two Bud Lights," I tell Turtle.

"Coming right up," he replies.

"Chase," Maddox says when he steps up to me at the bar. "Torin needs to see you."

"Fuck," I mutter. Not ready to let my brother meet Sasha yet, I ask her, "Will you be okay up here?"

"Yeah, sure. Go," she says. "I'll be fine. I'm a big girl."

"I know, but I'll have Maddox stay with you," I tell her.

"I don't need a babysitter, Chase," she groans, hopping up on the bar stool with a roll of her blue eyes.

"Don't let her out of your sight," I warn Maddox before I give Sasha a quick kiss on the lips.

...

Sasha

"If looks could kill," I murmur to Maddox between sips of my bottle of beer. "Well, then I think you and I would both be dead; you simply because of your proximity to me."

"The claws are definitely gonna come out," he agrees before he spins around on his stool when three blonde women walk up to me. I'm pretty sure that my flimsy shirt has more material than the three of their outfits combined. One is wearing a fishnet stocking dress, for chrisssakes, which means her nipples are poking out two of the holes.

"Can I help you, ladies?" I ask with my most pleasant, friendly reporter smile in place.

"Don't get your hopes up, honey," the fishnet chick says. "If Chase Fury takes you downstairs, it's just for you to suck his dick. Doesn't mean you're special."

"Oh," I say with a nod, trying to bite back my jealousy. They may have been with Chase before, but never again. This afternoon I got a call from D.C. letting me know that I got the correspondent job. I didn't tell Chase, because I'm going to turn it down. They gave me a few days to think about it, but I finally feel like I'm where I'm supposed to be. So, I better set these women straight, because I'm not going anywhere.

"Well," I start. "Since I took care of sucking his dick a few hours ago, he's probably all good, but thanks for your concern."

Beside me, I'm pretty sure Maddox spews a little of Chase's beer that he took over.

"See, that's all he's looking for, sweetie," the girl in a black leather dress with a silver zipper unzipped down to her navel says. "It's not a good sign if he left you up here. That means you're fair game for the other brothers. He won't even remember your name tomorrow. Hell, he's probably already forgotten it."

"Wanna bet?" I ask.

"Bet what?" the third slut asks.

"When he comes back, I'll prove you all wrong," I tell them. "Do you really want to embarrass yourselves? Wouldn't you rather go find someone else's dick to suck?"

"Wow, what a bitch," leather dress girl mutters under her breath.

I look at each woman one at a time and then the rest of the bar, most of whom are watching our little drama unfold, and I realize something. Setting down my bottle on the bar, I stand up, towering over all three of them, because I'm over six feet tall when I'm wearing my high heels.

"I get it now," I tell them. "Congrats, girls. You were the best Chase could do when he was trying to find my replacement. But that's all you'll ever be to him, and I can't wait to see the look on your faces when you realize it."

CHAPTER TWENTY

Chase

"WHAT'S UP?" I ASK TORIN, WHO IS SITTING IN HIS USUAL SEAT at the head of the table. I'm starting to realize he's spending way too much time here.

"I need to ask a favor," he says.

"Okay?" I say. Since I'm in a hurry, I don't take a seat, hoping he'll get to it. I should've brought Sasha down here with me. The club girls can be catty; but at the same time, Torin still thinks of her as nothing but a nosy reporter.

"Can I borrow some money?" Torin asks through gritted teeth, telling me it cost him his pride to ask me that.

"How much?"

"Four hundred," he says, and I know he means four hundred thousand.

"So a million dollars is what Hector wants from you?" I guess, since Kennedy said he took six hundred out of their account.

"How the fuck did you know that?" Torin asks.

"A little detective work," I reply. "And you know I'll give it to you, but it won't end there. Hector is gonna keep asking you for more money."

"I fucking know that, okay? That's what he's been doing for months. But what choice do I have?"

"Set the meet and then kill him," I suggest.

"I told you that I couldn't do that."

"Then you're fucked," I say, because it's true. "And we both know what he's gonna want after you pay him – you to hand me over to him."

Torin shakes his head. "I won't fucking do that."

"He's already asked, hasn't he?" I realize. God, I'm slow sometimes.

"Yes."

"Fucking great," I grumble as I cover my face. "I'm tired of sitting around and waiting for the other shoe to drop," I tell him. "Tonight, I'm putting together a crew, and then we're gonna track this shit down that he's blackmailing you with."

Torin takes a deep breath, and I know he's going to argue. He suddenly lets it out in a long sigh. "You should know what you're looking for. It's a video. It's not on a computer, though. Reece has already been getting into Hector's systems to check. He thinks it's probably on a flash drive somewhere. Hector knows I can't control you and expects you to keep causing trouble. If you do this, you better do it quietly," Torin finally warns me.

"I will. But you need to put everyone on notice. War is coming, and everyone needs to get ready. I'm gonna have Sasha stay here with the prospects tomorrow if we can set it up by then. You probably should get Kennedy to come in too. Will you stay here with them?"

"Yes," he agrees.

"Don't give Sasha any shit either, Torin. You can't point any fingers except at yourself for this mess."

"I fucking know that!" he shouts.

"Good," I say before I head back upstairs.

...

Sasha

"HEY, SWEETHEART, YOU DOIN' okay?" Chase asks when he returns and looks back and forth between the clueless girls and me.

"Yeah," I assure him, turning to kiss him in greeting. Running my hands up underneath his shirt that's covered by his cut, I ask, "Can I show them?"

He gives me a small smile and nods in understanding. I pull my hands out of his shirt to slip his cut off his shoulders, and then I grab the hem of his shirt and pull it over his head. The women gasp before he even turns for them to see the tattoo, like seeing Chase shirtless is something new.

"Better?" he asks me with a grin as I rub my palms up his abs and over his chest.

"Much," I reply. "Now just one more thing."

"What's that?" he asks.

"Could you please tell these ladies my name?"

Smirking, he lifts an eyebrow and says to them, "This is Sasha Eleanor Sheridan, my high school sweetheart. And I'm hoping she'll be my old lady."

Grinning so broadly my face may split, I remind Chase, "I already said yes ten years ago."

Nodding, Chase says, "Damn right you did." Then, he takes my hand and lifts it to his lips.

As he kisses my knuckles, the three cycle sluts stare stone-faced, then begin to slowly back away.

Before they can disappear into the throng of people in the bar,

Chase stands up straight and roars to be heard over the jukebox. "You hear that brothers? Meet my old lady!"

All of the club members, and most of the other men in the bar, raise their glasses or bottles and cheer as Chase kisses my hand again.

"Just as a friendly reminder to everyone," Chase continues, staring down each of the three girls who are still backing away. "That means any insult to Sasha is an insult to me, and by extension the Savage Kings. Now, Turtle, pour everyone a round on the house!"

The hollering and applause swells even louder at that proclamation, as Chase wraps me into his arms and brings me close for a kiss. We're jostled and slapped in congratulations by his brothers as they step to the bar, but nothing can distract us now that we have found each other once more. After an all too short period, Chase breaks away from me.

"I'm going to need you to hang out here with Maddox just a little longer, okay? I've gotta run downstairs and handle something, then we can have our drink."

I nod and take my seat back at the bar as he turns away, then raise my bottle briefly to the three girls staring dumbfounded as my old man disappears back into the basement of the club.

CHAPTER TWENTY-ONE

Chase

ONCE I'M BACK DOWNSTAIRS, I HEAD TO THE END OF THE HALL, where one of my quietest, and arguably most dangerous brothers, has his room. Before I can lift my hand to knock, he is already peering out of the cracked door, opening it fully when he sees me.

"Thought I heard someone coming my way," Reece says with a slight smile. His room is dark, except for a flickering of neon lights, which give his clean-shaven face an eerie backlight.

"Yo, Reece. Good to see you, man. I need your help," I tell our IT guy without further preamble. Reece isn't a man who likes to waste words or time.

"What do you need?" he asks, standing aside and waving me into his room. I glance around his apartment, which is probably as sterile as his former barracks. He's got a military cot in one corner, crisply made, and a desk near the back wall that faces the door. The only light in the room glows from the three large computer monitors. Thick bundles of zip-tied wiring sprout from the only other furniture in the room; some sort of shelf, which has a bunch of glowing boxes;

and a giant air conditioning unit blasting freezing air on them. The room is colder than the city morgue, but Reece doesn't seem to be bothered as he strides back over to his chair and pushes his back to the far wall.

"Can you get me the name and location of one of Hector Cruz's men? Not the bottom soldiers, but one of his commanders?"

Reece waves for me to step over behind his desk with him. As I move closer, I can see that his three monitors all seem to be streaming video of different businesses and residences.

"Torin asked me to keep tabs on Cruz and his crew after your incident the other day," Reece explains, nodding towards the screens. "I logged myself into a bunch of their security networks to analyze their operations and look for their daily patterns."

Reece leans back in his chair, staring at a blank spot on the wall. I've seen him do this before when he's cooking up a plan, and I know better than to interrupt him. I wait patiently, listening to the hum of the electronics around us until Reece suddenly leans over his keyboard and begins rapidly tapping on the keys.

"Your best target will be Malcolm Butner," Reece explains, zooming in on a video feed of what appears to be the front porch of a small residence. "You met him the other day. You shot his soldier, Keith Washington, on the highway. Malcolm broke his leg and arm when the truck rolled. His other soldier, Derek Sutton, broke an arm. They are both staying at this residence while they recover. Cruz has assigned another soldier to guard the house."

"Oh yeah, Abe bloodied that fucker's nose," I say when I recognize the face. "You got a quiet way in for me?" I ask, knowing that Reece is already mentally hammering out the details.

"Several options," Reece says under his breath, leaning back in his chair again before looking up at me. "One would be to get you a key to the house; let you walk right in while they sleep."

"How long would that take?" I ask him.

"One of Abe's old associates is now a locksmith. I would have to have him on standby until everyone left the house. With their injuries, that could be days."

"I need an in by tomorrow night," I clarify.

Reece goes blank again for a moment, staring back at the wall. He surprises me when he looks back up abruptly and asks, "Is Sparky here?"

"Sparky? Fast Eddie's bulldog? That Sparky?" I ask in confusion.

"You'll need Sparky," Reece says with a nod. Motioning back to the monitors, he clicks on the mouse to cycle through the security feeds inside the house where Malcolm Butner is staying. "I've been watching this house. It's isolated, but there are neighbors behind them, through some woods. The neighbors have dogs. Malcolm Butner appears to despise animals. The last two nights, he has sent his bodyguard outside to chase off the dogs when he hears them barking near the house."

I catch on to Reece's plan quickly, and it's brilliant in its simplicity. "Sparky is a noisy little shit. We take him around back, pop the soldier when he comes out to chase him off, then go on in before Malcolm or his boy can call for backup," I fill in, as Reece nods along.

"Take two burners. Call me on one, I can monitor the interior and tell you where Malcolm and Derek are at precisely. When you approach, I'll disable the cameras." Reece reaches under the desk as a printer whirs into motion, then hands me a sheet of paper. "Address," he concludes, then stands up to walk me back to the door.

"Thanks, brother," I tell him, clapping him on the shoulder. I'm glad that I can spend tonight with Sasha rather than torturing someone for information. I need a little time to put together my crew and get a few tools. I know Abe will be up for it. My boy, Sax, is kind of high-strung, but he'd laugh in the face of the devil. Our enforcer, Miles, is an expert at getting information out of people, and of course, I'll have to bring Eddie along with Sparky.

Back upstairs I return to the bar where Sasha asks, "Everything okay?"

"Yeah," I tell her, kissing her on the cheek. "Let's call it a night. Come downstairs with me?"

"I was warned you may take me down to give you a blowjob," she says, making me bark out a laugh.

"I need some time to recover from the one earlier today," I reply.

"That's what I told them!" she says with a grin as she grabs my cut and t-shirt that I left earlier and hops off the stool.

I'm glad to see that the club girls aren't getting to her. I know it's not easy for Sasha to be here around them, knowing I've slept with a few. But she doesn't have anything to worry about now. I'm done with other women for good.

Downstairs, I let Sasha into my room.

"Are the sheets clean?" she asks.

"Yes," I assure her.

"Good."

On the way to the bathroom, I tell Sasha, "Get naked," before I go take a piss in my adjoining bathroom.

When I come back, removing my jeans as I go, I stop short when I see Sasha kneeling on my bed...wearing nothing but my cut.

"That's it," I tell her before I continue removing my shoes and pants. "That's the only thing I want you to wear from now on."

Sasha laughs and asks, "But then what would I do when you're wearing it?"

Climbing up on the bed in front of her, I tell her, "I guess you'll just have to be naked."

Her arms go around my neck as I pull her onto my lap. "Are we really doing this?" she asks.

"Doing what?" I reply, since I'm assuming she's not talking about fucking.

"Us. Are we back together? I mean, is this really what you want? Me to be your old lady? Should we date first?"

"We've already dated," I remind her. "I wanted to make you mine before everything happened. That's still what I want."

"I love my job," she says. "But if we go public, then the station may let me go."

"Because I'm a wanted biker?" I ask.

"Yeah. Not exactly good PR if I officially associate with the Kings."

"I don't want you to lose your job," I tell her. "I know you're doing what you love and that you wanted to travel. But I can't leave the club either."

"I know that," she says. "I could give it up for you."

"You shouldn't have to," I say, not wanting her to lose anything because of me again.

"No, I shouldn't. But if it comes down to you or my career, well, I've had my career for six years, and it hasn't made me as happy as the last few days with you have."

Damn, she knows how to bring a man to his knees.

"I'll start my own news station if I have to," I assure her. "You can be the official MC reporter or help with the club's PR. We're gonna need it after my patch was IDed in that shootout on the highway."

"We'll see," Sasha replies. "I just needed to know if we were on the same page about the future."

"Our future is together. That's all I know for sure," I say while brushing my lips against hers. "I love you. Always have. Always will."

"I love you too," she replies.

...

Sasha

WHEN I WAKE up the next morning, Chase is already sitting on the edge of the bed talking quietly on his phone. I roll over and scoot closer to him, laying my head against his broad back. When I reach around his waist, he pats my hand absently. The longer I listen to his conversation the more puzzled I become.

"Cut the jumper cables and rewire them to plug into a standard electric socket. Yeah, like the Cartel uses, exactly," Chase says. "Also, get me four wood clamps, but sharpen the screws. Nah, I've got the burners. The only other thing we need you to bring is Sparky. Yeah, bro, I said bring Sparky. Something to get him excited too, you know, get him barking? Of course he's not going to get hurt, Eddie! Meet us here at the clubhouse after you get done at the garage, okay? All right, brother, see you then."

Ending the call, Chase drops the phone beside him on the bed. "What was all that about?" I ask him, moving up to press my lips into his shoulder.

"Just making arrangements for tonight. I'm going to take some of the boys out to talk with Hector's crew; try to get some of this shit resolved."

I can feel him tensing up, and I know what he's thinking. That I'll try to talk him out of this. I hug him fiercely from behind and then whisper directly into his ear, "You come back to me safe, Chase Fury. Do what needs to be done, but you come back to me unharmed, understand?"

He turns towards me with a smile, and his posture relaxes. "You know I'm going to be fine, sweetheart. I want you to hang out here tonight. What kind of plans do you have today?"

"Right now, I'm planning on brushing my teeth," I tell him as I shift onto my knees, pressing my breasts into his back. "Then, I'm planning to come back and take you for a ride of my own."

Chase laughs; and when I climb off the bed, heading for the bathroom, he swats me on the ass as I squirm out of his reach. Once I've gotten myself cleaned up a bit, I open the bathroom door to find him already stretched out across the bed, naked, with all the sheets kicked down to the floor.

"I'm ready to ride, how about you?" he asks playfully.

Instead of answering, I just grin at him and stalk over to the bed, grabbing his legs and crawling up his body until my hair drags across his semi-hard cock. He shivers and gathers it up in one hand, holding it out of my face as I take him into my mouth. Chase groans as he begins to swell while I work.

After only a couple of minutes, he grabs my shoulders, surprising me as he tugs me up his body, smashing his lips to mine. Reaching down between us to align our bodies, I slam myself down onto him, unable to wait another second for him to possess me.

Our kiss breaks as we both gasp at the initial sensation of him invading me. Chase's hands grip my tits as he pushes me back and I begin to grind my hips on him. The first orgasm slams through me so intensely that my pussy clamps down on him, locking us together.

Before I can completely recover, Chase has pulled me back down to him, one hand entwined in my hair as he kisses me roughly, the other digging into my ass as he begins guiding my movements up and down his shaft. Every few strokes, as our bodies slap together, I rock my hips, grinding my clit against him. I lose track of time as waves of pleasure rock me over and over again, lost to everything except the feeling of this beautiful man beneath me.

I have no idea how long we've been mauling each other when Chase suddenly wraps an arm around my lower back and digs his fingers even deeper into my ass. Pressing his heels into the bed to lift me up slightly, his cock begins hammering at me desperately, breaking our rhythm. His frantic pace sends me screaming over the edge one last time as I feel the hot surge of his cum erupting into me.

I collapse on top of him as he finally slows, gasping for breath. Now I'm glad that Chase kicked off all the sheets, as our sweat is actually making our chests stick together. Laughing, we peel ourselves apart and head to the shower to scrub each other down.

Once we towel off, I get to work drying my hair while Chase disappears upstairs. By the time I'm done, he's returned to his apartment with a stack of peanut butter and jelly sandwiches and a huge bag of chips.

"Best I could do right now, sweetheart," he says as we sit on the bed together and dig in.

"I'm here for the company, not the cuisine. You make a really sloppy sandwich!" I tease, after a huge glob of jelly falls out and lands between my tits since I'm still naked. A moment later, Chase has his head buried in my cleavage, cleaning me up and sending me into a fit of giggles.

After we eat, we lay on the bed holding each other, and I think Chase even naps for a while. He startles awake when there's a knock on the door. Rubbing at his eyes, he struggles to his feet and pulls on a pair of jeans to go answer it while I hide myself under the sheets.

"Kennedy!" Chase says in surprise, throwing the door open wide. "Meet Sasha. Sasha, this is Torin's old lady."

"Hello, lovebirds!" Kennedy grins as she leans into the room. "I heard you had some things to do tonight, Chase, and wanted to see if Sasha might want to come shopping with me."

"What do you think, sweetheart?" Chase asks me.

"Of course, that's a great idea," I tell her. "Just give me a moment to get straightened up. I'll be right back."

Chase and Kennedy step out into the doorway so that I can duck into the bathroom to dress in one of the outfits I packed — jeans and a pink blouse. Even in the bathroom I'm still able to hear Chase telling Kennedy, "Thank you. It'll be good for you guys to spend some time together, and it will keep her from worrying about things tonight."

"Torin mentioned that you had a 'special run' tonight, but he wouldn't tell me anything else. I'm sure it must be something dangerous, but I know you'll be careful. Remember everything you have here, and don't take any crazy chances." Kennedy laughs, then says, "Oh, I might as well tell the sun not to rise in the morning. Don't worry about Sasha. We'll just be getting into a little trouble of our own."

Dressed and ready, I grab my purse and then open the door to let Kennedy and Chase know I'm all set.

Chase kisses me goodbye, and he assures me he'll be back later tonight. With a groan, Kennedy leads me up the stairs back to the bar, moving slowly in the late stages of her pregnancy.

"So, what do you have in mind this evening?" I ask her, knowing that her options are a bit limited right now.

"You have no idea how glad I am you're here," Kennedy grins back at me over her shoulder. "Torin hates Chinese food, and I have been craving it for weeks. I can do take-out, of course, but it's time I had a buffet buddy. There is nothing in this world lonelier than going to the Chinese buffet alone."

"A Chinese buffet? You really do like to live dangerously," I say when I laugh with her. "Come on, let's go see what we can get into."

Kennedy drives us to what she calls a 'hidden gem,' Captain Chen's seafood and oriental buffet. "Oh, girl, are you sure about this?" I ask her one last time before we enter.

"Yes! You know as well as I do, life is all about taking chances. If you end up regretting it, just think of how I must be feeling and remember that you humored a pregnant woman."

Nodding, I hold the door open for her and follow her inside.

After we get settled down in our booth with our plates full, I have to admit that Kennedy's cravings paid off. "This place is amazing!" I gush, cracking open a crab leg.

"Thank you again for coming with me," Kennedy replies. "It feels good to get out with another woman who isn't...well, you know how the girls at the clubhouse can be."

"I've gotten a little taste of it," I say wryly, waving the crab meat before I take a bite.

"I wanted you to know how happy I am for you, and especially Chase. He's my brother-in-law, and I've known him for years. I never understood why he looked so...lost until earlier when I saw the way he looked at you..." Kennedy begins to tear up and grabs her napkin to wipe at her eyes. "Stupid pregnancy hormones," she apologizes.

"What was he like...you know, while we were apart?" I ask her, once she regains her composure.

"Ugh, well...he's always difficult, you know that. But he was so angry, at nothing in particular. I mean, never to me, but ask any of his brothers and they'll tell you. They never knew what word or look might set him off. It even became sort of a rite of passage amongst prospects. Some brother would set them up to ask Chase about his tattoo, and they would see how long they could stand toe-to-toe with Chase raging at them."

"He would hit someone just for asking about me?" I ask her, shocked.

"It wasn't just that they asked, not really. I talked to him about it once, when he had been drinking and seemed calmer than usual. He told me that every time someone asked him, all the regret, the shame, and the pain he felt losing you, it all just came boiling back out. He just couldn't stand it, and he took it out on whoever brought it up."

"But having you back with us," Kennedy continues as she shakes her head. "It's like night and day. He's been almost giddy, practically floating with every step he takes."

"I know how he feels," I tell her honestly. "The butterflies in my stomach could possibly carry me away. I missed him so damned much, and the pain of being without him...well, I never hit anyone at least."

"Hey, I want you to know, too, that these last few days are unusual. This isn't how the club operates, at least never in my experience. These guys are rough, but day to day they run a legitimate network of businesses up and down the strip here," Kennedy assures me with a pat to my arm.

"Other than the weed thing?" I ask with an arched eyebrow.

She waves that off, saying, "That will be legal in a couple of years. These guys are just getting out in front of the next big opportunity." She grins at me slyly, "That's what they're pushing their local representative for, anyway. They're more politically active than you may expect, in some regards. Who knows, Torin or Chase might be mayor one day."

I almost choke on my fried rice at that idea, and we both fall into a fit of giggling that forces us to go to the bathroom. We end up spending over two hours at Captain Chen's, swapping stories about the men that have become central to both our lives.

When Kennedy drops me off at the clubhouse later on that evening, I lean over her belly to give her a huge hug, feeling like she's become such a good friend in such a short amount of time.

"I'm so glad you're here," she tells me. "And I can't wait for everything to settle down and my little man to arrive, so we can finally get back to being a family."

"I can't wait to meet him, and I'm so excited to be here for this," I assure her. "You head home and get some rest. If you feel like I do, you probably need to lie down for a while!"

After another hug, I head into the bar, knowing it's too early for Chase to be back. Noticing that several of the brothers, including Abe are also absent, I take a seat by the bar and settle in to wait, trying to assure myself that the heavy weight I feel in my chest is just from our overindulgent dinner.

CHAPTER TWENTY-TWO

Chase

After Sasha and Kennedy head out, I go upstairs to wait on my boys to arrive. Abe is already there, throwing darts with Sax. Miles is sitting at the bar, watching a baseball game. I go sit down beside him while we wait for Fast Eddie to bring the van and the dog.

"You ready for tonight?" I ask Miles as I take the stool beside him.

He grunts, then knocks back the shot sitting in front of him. He pours two more from a bottle of Jim Beam he has at hand, and slides one over to me. "For luck," he rumbles, tossing it back.

I raise my glass to him, then lean in close after I swallow. "Abe give you the run down on tonight?" I ask quietly.

"Bit of wet-work, if I understand correctly," he confirms.

"Just a little," I assure him. "Three guys we have to deal with; two of them are injured."

"Bah, you barely need me then. You're bringing a flamethrower to a backyard barbecue," he says.

"Hell, brother, I knew we could handle it without you. But me and the boys didn't want you getting bored. We figured you could use the excitement."

With a toothy grin, Miles looks over to the door. "Looks like our ride is here," he says, nodding to Fast Eddie. "I appreciate you calling on me, Chase. Even if it's an easy job, it means a lot to me to work with you."

"Abe, Sax, let's roll," I yell as I head for the door. "You ready to ride, Eddie? Got the stuff?" I ask him.

"Yeah, Sparky's in the van, and I put together the stuff you asked for. You, uh...you're not gonna make *me* use those things, are you?" Eddie asks nervously.

"No way, man, the guy those are intended for is all mine. Don't you worry about that," I assure him.

Eddie nods to Miles and the other brothers as we all head back outside. "Let's go grab a burger on the way," Eddie suggests. "Once it's a bit later and they're settled in, this should be an easy job."

"You sure you want to eat before something like this?" Sax asks Eddie.

"Shit, never mind," Eddie replies glumly. "Come on, let's get this over with."

...

WE PARK the van several miles away from the house where Malcolm Butner is staying, and I call Reece on the burner. "What's it look like in there, man?" I ask him.

"As expected," Reece replies shortly. "Malcolm has just been helped into bed by one of his men. He is upstairs, second room on the left. The man who helped him into bed is in the bedroom straight down the hall. The soldier on watch is downstairs watching television in the front room. Sutton, the other injured guy, left and hasn't been back, but I've seen no one else enter or leave."

"Good deal, brother. It's time. Cut their security feeds and stay near your phone. We'll call you when we're done." I close the phone and nod to Eddie, who is looking back at me from the driver's seat. "Park about a block down the street, and let's get this done."

A few minutes later, Eddie lets out a nervous laugh, killing the lights on the van just as the house comes into view. "Activate cloaking device," he chortles. "We're going in dark."

"What the fuck are you on about, man?" Sax asks him. "Park this bitch and let's go."

Sparky looks up from the floorboards and whines as Eddie kills the engine. "This ain't the park, buddy, but you might get to play a bit." Gathering up the bulldog in his arms, he digs into a bag beside him and pulls out a well-chewed plush groundhog.

"What's that for?" Abe asks, nodding towards the squeaky toy.

"I had to bring something to get him barking," Eddie explains. "Nothing gets him going faster than his humpy."

"His *humpy*?" Abe snickers.

Sparky is already eyeing the groundhog and growling softly. "Oh yeah, see? He's about to lose his shit already. Let's go before he starts rubbing his rocket on me."

Chuckling, I grab my bag of tools, and we all pile out of the van. "All right, Eddie, you and Sparky go around the left side of the house, like we planned. Miles, you go with him. Get Sparky going; and when the dude comes out, Miles will take care of him. Abe and Sax, you're with me. We'll be on the right side and back you up if anything goes wrong. Eddie, after we're in, you bring Sparky back to the van and keep watch."

Everyone gives their agreement before we pull ski masks over our faces, then cross the yard to hustle into our positions. Reece had told us there were neighbors through the woods behind the house, but the place is fairly isolated, with no other surrounding homes.

Once Abe, Sax, and I are in position, we sit tight, listening as

Sparky begins growling and yipping from the other side of the house. Sax lets out a short, nervous giggle as we hear the 'humpy' begin to squeak furiously, just before Sparky erupts into a fit of furious barking.

"Madre de Dios!" we hear someone roar from inside the house. *"Esteban, go shut that dog up!"*

Sax slaps a hand over his mouth to stifle another burst of laughter, just before we hear the front door open and the porch light come on, illuminating the front yard. We're safely out of range around the house, but I can hear heavy footsteps on the stairs. I motion to Abe, who raises his pistol in preparation, just in case this dumb bastard comes around our side instead.

I didn't need to worry. Just a few seconds later, I hear *"Que mierda?"* just before two soft, hissing shots through the silencer and something heavy hitting the ground. "Let's go," I tell the brothers.

Miles is already at the foot of the stairs, pistol still in his hand, and Eddie is hustling back towards the van with Sparky cradled in his arms. With a quick nod to Miles, I take the lead, clearing the entrance and making sure to check behind the door for any surprises. Pointing to Sax, I signal for him to stay downstairs and watch the front before I lead Miles and Abe up the stairs.

I motion for Miles to take the door at the end of the hall, then Abe and I take positions outside Malcolm's room. On my signal, Abe kicks open the door, and I leap forward, gun levelled at the bed.

Malcolm Butner is propped up against some pillows in the dark room, his broken leg stretched out before him. His head snaps up as I enter, and his right arm fumbles instinctively for the gun on his bedside table. Terrible positioning for him, since his right arm is the one in the cast. He slaps his hand down on it futilely as I cross the room, smashing the butt of my gun across the bridge of his nose.

The asshole screams and sputters, trying to roll away from me as Abe secures the gun on the nightstand. Miles enters a moment later, smoke still rising from the silencer on his pistol. He nods to me, confirming that the house is now clear, and then comes over to help me as I throw some zip-ties from my tool bag onto the bed.

"Bring me a chair from the dining room," I order Abe, as I keep my gun pressed against the back of Malcolm's head. Abe nods and takes off, while Miles begins going through my bag, looking at the other implements I've brought with us.

"Hector's gonna fucking kill you," Malcolm spits, snorting through the blood still running out of his nose.

"Not tonight," Miles responds calmly. "Tonight is your special night. We are going to kill you. If you answer our questions, you die easy. If you don't want to answer them, then, well...your suffering will be legendary."

Malcolm freezes at the harsh threat, allowing me, Abe and Miles to easily zip-tie his leg and arms into position in the chair.

"You two head back downstairs," I order Miles and Abe once Malcolm is secured. Miles looks over the sharpened wood clamps he pulled from my bag, along with the modified jumper cables and the machete I packed.

"You sure you don't need me?" Miles asks. "Those tools are the kinds of things that give men nightmares. I'm not talking about the victims; I'm talking about the guys using them."

"I'm fine," I assure him. "This slimy little dickhead wants to hurt my family. I *want* to do this."

Nodding, Miles asks, "You still want us to set it up like a cartel hit?" Miles asks.

"Yeah. You guys go handle that. I'll be down after our conversation." I turn to Malcolm, whose eyes are practically bugging out of his head staring at my tools. I pull the last item out of my bag, a ball-gag, and hold it up to his face.

"Decision time, Malcolm," I say pleasantly. "Shall we talk, or shall I get to work?"

...

HALF AN HOUR later I head downstairs, weary and frustrated. Abe, Miles, and Sax are all gathered in the kitchen, keeping an eye out for any interruptions.

"You get what you need?" Abe asks when I appear. "Seems like it went pretty fast."

"We're done here," I tell them shortly. And without any further conversation, we jog back to the van. Sparky is in the shotgun seat, so we all pile into the back, breathing heavily as we finally pull off our ski masks. Eddie wastes no time driving off; and a few moments later, we're clear of the scene.

"All right, man, time to spill the beans," Abe says. "What was all this about tonight?"

With a heavy sigh, I look around at my brothers. "Torin's in trouble. Hector Cruz set his goons on me and Abe to remind Torin that he owes him some money. Hector's demanding Torin cough up a million dollars, or he's going to leak some sort of video showing our President doing...something. Torin's already coughed up no telling how much cash before now to that fucker."

"What the hell could Torin have done that's worth a million bucks to hide?" Abe asks.

"Torin won't tell me what it is. I had hoped Malcolm would know, but it looks like Hector is playing this close to his chest. It doesn't have anything to do with the cartel or their drugs. It's something Malcolm and their crew of traffickers aren't involved with. The only things Malcolm knew was that Hector has promised the Aces access to our fucking territory and that just two people are aware of what the shit with Torin is about - Hector, and for some reason, Hector's daughter, a chick named Lexi."

"If it's not about drugs," Miles says, "then Hector is going rogue and doing this without the cartel backing him up. They might not be happy that he's making plays on the side, without their involvement. And if only he and his daughter know what it is..."

"I'm not going to play any guessing games," I interrupt. "Torin's our president, and he wouldn't do anything intentionally to hurt this club. We'll figure this shit out together, and if it means taking down Hector and dealing with backlash from the cartel..."

"We'll make them regret even glancing at our territory," Abe finishes. "This is our town, and these drugs they're slinging are hurting our people. We'll make them bleed for every person they've hurt trying to muscle in on our home."

"You're damned right we will." I nod to Abe. "I just hope that we can shut them down before too many of us have to bleed with them."

CHAPTER TWENTY-THREE

Sasha

CHASE GOT HOME LATE LAST NIGHT; AND FROM WHAT I CAN tell, things didn't go as well as he'd hoped. Instead of staying in the clubhouse, he wanted us to come back to the farmhouse to have more privacy.

I asked if we could take his bike, and he gave me some excuse about a storm coming and how he didn't want us to get caught in it. I didn't press the issue but plan to bring it up again soon.

When both of our phones start going off early in the morning, I sneak out of bed and grab them both to take them downstairs, so Chase can get more sleep.

Since Debra, the station's producer, has called me twice, I go ahead and call her back.

"Hey, Debra, it's Sasha," I say.

"Sasha, how are you feeling? Any better?"

"Yes," I say to further the lie I told her yesterday when I called in sick. "Hopefully I can recover over the weekend and be back on Monday."

Honestly, I've enjoyed my break. It's nice not to worry about how I look or what hateful comments I'll get on social media about my outfits.

"Glad to hear you're on the mend," Debra says. "And congrats! World News Tonight called to get our referral for you and said you got the job!"

"I did," I reply. "But I don't think I'm going to take it."

"Really? I thought you were excited?"

"I was, but I'm happy here," I say, thinking of Chase upstairs in the bed.

"It's a big decision," Debra says. "We'll support you in whatever you decide."

"I appreciate that," I tell her.

"I'll let you go rest up," she says. "You're missing one helluva news day, though."

"Oh really?" I ask, curious and a little disappointed to miss out on the excitement. "What's going on?"

"You know the motorcycle gang that wears the bearded skull with a crown, the Savage Kings?"

"Yes," I say, not willing to tell her just how intimately I know them.

"There was a shooting outside their clubhouse, like a rival gang or something, and..."

"And?" I ask impatiently.

"A woman was shot."

"No," I gasp. Looking at the screen of Chase's phone, I see a list of missed call from several of his brothers. Fuck. "Who?" I ask Debra.

"They haven't released her name yet, but there are rumors she was one of the old ladies."

"Oh my God," I gasp when my breath is knocked out of my lungs and tears fill my eyes. "I-I have to go," I tell her before I end the call and run up the steps with both of our phones. "Chase," I say kneeling on my side of the bed to shake his shoulder "Chase, baby, wake up!" I urge as a sob leaves my throat.

"What's wrong, sweetheart?" he asks as he pops up, bleary-eyed in concern.

"There was a shooting...at the clubhouse." I open his hand and put his phone in it. He blinks at the list of missed calls and curses before his finger moves over the buttons, and he puts it up to his ear.

"Abe," he says. I'm close enough to hear Abe's response.

"It's bad man. We're at the hospital, but it's not looking good."

I slap my hand over my mouth in worry as Chase explodes, coming out of bed and pulling on his jeans with one hand with the phone between his shoulder and ear.

"What the fuck's going on? *Who's* at the hospital?" he shouts.

I can't hear Abe's response, but I know by the way Chase's back slumps against the wall that it's her.

Kennedy, Torin's wife, is in the hospital, and her and their baby are most likely fighting for their lives.

...

Chase

Thank fuck my body runs on automatic functions, or I'd be worthless.

Kennedy was shot by some stupid motherfucker right outside of our clubhouse. Abe said that, after the ambulance got her to the hospital, they took her back to surgery and they hadn't told Torin a damn thing in over an hour.

Sasha and I ran through the parking lot and into the surgical waiting room, looking for my brother. I knew that Torin was gonna be a wreck, but seeing him was even worse than I expected. He jumps up from his chair to throw his arms around me, and my throat clogs up with emotion when I see the blood soaking through his cut, his shirt, and his jeans.

"How is she?" I ask when he pulls back and wipes his eyes on the short sleeves of his tee.

"They won't tell me...they won't tell me *anything* about her or... or the baby," he says with a clenched jaw.

Clasping his shoulder, I tell him, "Kennedy is tough. She's a fighter, and I bet that kid of yours is too."

"Yeah," he replies with a nod. "Yeah, they are."

The guys make room for Sasha and me to sit next to Torin, Sasha's fingers squeezing mine while we all wait in silence. Torin can't sit still for long. He's up pacing most of the time.

I want to ask what the fuck happened, but now's not the time. If I had to guess, it had to have been Hector. Torin is probably blaming himself, and I know exactly how he feels. The waiting while Sasha was in surgery was the worst hours of my life. Hearing the doctor say she was in recovery and doing well was such a relief I nearly kissed the man.

"Get them the fuck out of here!" Torin shouts when he looks through the windows of the hospital and sees the media vans out front.

"On it," Sax says, jumping up to head outside.

"I can't believe this," Torin mutters to himself, scrubbing his hands across his face over and over again. "She has to be okay. She has to!"

"Mr. Fury?"

I swear the entire world stopped spinning in the seconds following the surgeon's appearance in the middle of the waiting room. Our whole group jumps to our feet as Torin stands frozen in place like he can't make himself walk over and talk to the man in blue scrubs who has answers for him. Thankfully, the surgeon comes to us instead. His face is solemn, not the least bit hopeful before he speaks.

"I'm so sorry," he tells Torin. "We did everything we could..."

"How is she?" Torin interrupts, still holding out hope, unable to accept the words as the doctor meant them.

"I'm sorry, but your wife's heart stopped while in transit. We tried to revive her and deliver your son. We couldn't save either of them."

"No!" Torin gasps. "No, please, God, no!"

"I'm so sorry for your losses," the surgeon says again, then walks away as if he didn't just drop the atomic bomb that annihilated everything that was good in my brother's life.

Torin falls to his knees and buries his head in his hands as he starts to sob. I kneel down beside him and wrap my arms around him as tears overflow from my eyes.

I can't believe Kennedy is gone. It just...it doesn't seem possible that something so awful could happen to someone so good. And the poor baby...

There's no way that my brother will ever be able to recover from this. But as soon as he has a chance to grieve, heads are gonna fucking roll, and I'll be right there with him, swinging the ax.

...

Sasha

DEATH IS nothing new for me. As a reporter, I've seen all kinds of horrible tragedies, the worst moments in all sorts of lives.

But this, being here at the hospital with Chase when the doctor gave the devastating news to Torin that his wife and baby are gone is more painful than anything I've ever experienced. Maybe because I know the news is also hurting the man I love.

I didn't even know Kennedy that well, only spoke to her once when we went to dinner, but still, my heart is breaking because she was such a sweet woman and didn't deserve to have her life taken so soon.

The entire packed waiting room remains frozen, most of us crying silently as we listen to Torin's heartbreaking sobs. And at this moment, when his entire life has been turned upside down, all of his men surround him placing a hand on his back or shoulder or arm to show him their respect and condolences, their solidarity.

This is what the MC is about. Some people think that these guys are nothing but outlaws, broken men with criminal backgrounds who break the law for sport. The other half is made up of military veterans suffering from post-traumatic stress, unable to fit in with the regular world after their return from war, so they decide to make their own rules. But really, the Savage Kings MC is about a loyal brotherhood made up of men on the outskirts of society who support each other through the good times and the bad.

And I know as I look at their united group that one thing is clear – whoever hurts one member, hurts them all. They'll find the gunman, and then there will be bloodshed. While I may not agree with their methods, I can agree that someone needs to inflict justice for such an awful crime.

I just hope that Chase doesn't end up getting himself killed or arrested.

Things are going to get bad until the MC enacts their revenge. People will get hurt, some may die. Even knowing all of that, I couldn't leave Chase now, not after all the time apart and how amazing it feels to be with him again. Through whatever may come, I'll be here, by his side when he needs me.

Hopefully, that won't be seeing him behind bars or in the morgue.

Chase stands up and breaks free from the group of men first. He wipes his face on the hem of his shirt before he turns around and faces me.

I meet him halfway, wrapping my arms around his neck as he squeezes me to him tightly.

"I'm so sorry, baby," I whisper, unable to figure out the right words to make things better. There aren't any; I don't think. So I just hold him until he pulls away.

"I'm, um, I'm gonna talk to the doctors," he says. "See if they'll let Torin go back and see her."

"Okay," I agree. "Do you need me to do anything?" I ask.

He shakes his head. "I need to call my dad before he hears about it on television. I'll go outside and do that; then I'll find a nurse or doctor."

"Let me try to do that part. I'll find someone who can let Torin go back and wait for you to return," I say. "But don't go outside. There are still news vans and all out there."

"Oh, yeah, you're right. I didn't think about that," Chase says as he presses the heels of his hands into his eyes. "This is just so...I don't even know what to say..."

"I know," I agree, giving him another hug around his waist. "I'm here, whatever you need. I'm not going anywhere."

"Thanks, sweetheart," he says. "I'll be right back."

With a nod, I walk with him to the information desk. Chase goes down the hall a little further to an empty corridor to pull out his phone.

"Excuse me," I say to the woman behind the counter. "Mr. Fury just received the news that his wife and newborn son passed away. Could you please find out if he can go back to see them? His brother is right there down the hall and would like to take him," I explain as I point out Chase.

"Oh, of, course. I'm so sorry for your loss," she says, looking behind me to the group of men in leather still huddled around each other. "Let me make a few calls, and I'll let you know as soon as I find out."

"Great, thank you," I tell her before I start down the hallway toward Chase. I have a feeling that he'll need a little support during this conversation.

"Torin and I are fine," he tells his father. "But, um, listen, Kennedy was the one who got hurt."

Placing my hand on the center of Chase's cut, I rub his back as he tries to find the words. "She...she didn't make it, Dad. The baby didn't either."

I can't imagine how hard it is for Chase to be the one to have to deliver that horrible news to his father.

"I know, I know," he says with a sniffle in response to whatever his father says. "How do you think he is? We need you here. Yeah, we're at the hospital. Okay. Love you, too. Bye."

Ending the call, Chase says, "They're on the way."

"Good," I say when I lay my head on his back. I know he probably doesn't like me seeing him cry.

"Fuck," he mutters as he bows his head and covers it with his hands. "I don't think I've ever heard my father cry before today."

"Everyone is hurting," I explain. "There's not much worse that can happen to anyone."

"Yeah," he agrees. Taking a few deep breaths, Chase turns around and pulls me into his side and places a kiss on the top of my head. "I'm so glad you're here. I'd be lost without you to keep me standing when it feels like the ground under my feet is all crumbling apart."

"We'll get through this," I tell him. "One small step at a time."

He must nod, because I feel his chin move against my head before it returns.

"They're working on getting Torin back there to see her," I say.

"God fucking help us," he mutters.

...

Chase

"Mr. Fury? We can take you back now," a nurse in green scrubs says when she comes out into the lobby.

"War?" I ask, tilting my chin toward the nurse because I want him to help me get Torin back there. This isn't gonna be pretty, and hell, it'll probably be even worse than getting the news, but my brother needs this, to see her and say goodbye. I know he does, even though I wish we could be anywhere else right now.

War gives a nod of understanding and then, one of us on each side, pull my brother to his feet.

"Wh-what are you doing? Where are we...where we going?" Torin asks as we start guiding him down the hallway.

"Don't you want to see her?" I ask.

"No," he answers, and then, "Yes, but I don't know if I can yet."

His voice breaks on the last word, and it's like a goddamn chainsaw cuts off my knees. I power through because my brother needs me right now. I've got to be the strong one today, holding him up and helping him get through this shit. That's what he would do for me.

"We've got you," I tell him, looking over his slumped body to War. It takes him a few moments to visually swallow down his emotions. He's the only one of us who has a kid and a former old lady, so I'm guessing that this is all hitting pretty close to home today.

"We're here for you, brother," War says to Torin. "Every step of the way, every second of the day. Don't doubt that for an instant, no matter how bad things get."

With a nod, Torin continues to follow the nurse down the hallway, needing only a little bit of support from War and me when he stumbles. Rather than having too much to drink, he's had too much goddamn heartbreak today to put one boot in front of the other.

Slowly, though, we make it to our destination – also known as hell on Earth.

I go in first and see Kennedy lying on the bed, so peaceful that it looks like she could just be sleeping, except that her face is pale and her lips are a little blue. Then, I spot the bassinet, and it's too fucking much.

Strong. I have to be strong. Because a second after me, Torin walks in and sucks in a deep breath.

"Oh, God," he whispers as he goes over to Kennedy. He lifts her head and cradles it to his chest as he bawls on her. "What did they do to you, baby? What did they do?" he cries.

War rests his hand on my shoulder when I start to move forward. "Give him some time," he says. "He needs to say goodbye. We'll be here when he's ready."

Nodding in agreement, I let him turn me around to step back into the hallway where he pulls the door closed.

With my back pressed against the wall, I slide down it until my ass hits the floor to bury my face in my hands. God, when will these fucking tears stop?

War sits down next to me.

"What the fuck happened?" I ask, needing to know.

"I dunno much," he says. "We'll need to call Jade..."

"I'm guessing she'll be here as soon as she can," I tell him.

"All I know is that I saw Kennedy bring Torin some breakfast. He'd been at the table working when I came in around six," he says. "I knew he'd be there early, and I didn't want him there alone with everyone else asleep. I've had this feeling in my gut, you know?"

"Yeah, I know," I reply, familiar with that same ache that tells you shit's about to go sideways.

"Torin was pacing, stressed when Kennedy came in. She stayed and ate a biscuit or whatever with him, while I shot some pool. Then, she left..." He pauses a moment and then says, "We could hear the gun shots even through the soundproofing. When we all got upstairs and out to the parking lot, Kennedy was on the ground, bleeding from two bullet wounds, one in her chest and one in her fucking stomach like..."

"Like they meant to take the baby's life too," I finish for him through gritted teeth.

War nods. "We called an ambulance and tried to put pressure on her to stop the bleeding. The paramedics got there within four or five minutes and rushed her here."

"So you think she was the intended target?" I ask.

"Hell yes. There was no one else around. If the assholes wanted to hurt us, they would've waited until night when the bar and parking lot was full, then sprayed us with bullets," War explains. "This was intentional. It was a message."

"Fucking Hector Cruz," I mutter.

"Why, though? Because of those guys of his that you took out? Why would he fucking do this shit to Kennedy and not you or your girl?"

My jaw nearly breaks as I think about how it could've easily been Sasha lying cold in that bed.

"Torin owes Hector money," I confide in War.

"Bullshit," he replies without delay.

"He does. Blackmail money. Torin admitted it to me the other day, but he didn't want to bring it to the table."

"Holy shit," War curses under his breath. "You should've come to me and told me, Chase! It's my fucking job to keep Torin alive!"

"I know," I admit. "I should have, but he told me he was handling it. I never thought it would get this bad."

"Jesus Christ," he mutters. "And now we're going to war."

"No doubt," I agree.

The two of us sit there in silence as we both consider the ramifications of what happened today, what this means for the future.

There will be bloodshed. More death. It's inevitable. No one kills the fucking old lady of an MC president and gets away with it. Torin's gonna want to take out Hector's entire organization, and all of his brothers will be right there by his side, pulling the triggers.

After nearly an hour has passed, I get to my feet and tell War, "We need to get him out of here."

I know my brother, and if I had to guess, it won't be long before his grief turns into anger. I don't want him to be in the middle of the fucking hospital when he starts destroying shit.

"You're right. Let's get him to the clubhouse," War agrees when he stands up too. "He doesn't need to be alone. I'll put both of the prospects on him and keep an eye on him myself tonight."

"Good idea," I agree.

He pulls out his phone to notify the boys, and I push open the door to the room.

Inside, Torin is sitting in one of the chairs, holding his son.

Without looking up at me, Torin says, "He didn't deserve this."

"No, he didn't," I agree.

"They were completely innocent, and he took them just to hurt me." His words are said through his clenched jaw. The anger is rising, just like I expected.

"I know you don't want to, but it's time to say goodbye," I tell him.

With a nod, Torin squeezes his eyes shut before he leans down and kisses the forehead of his son. Then, he stands up and places the forever sleeping baby back into his bed.

"I wanna hit Hector tonight," he says when he's in front of me.

"No."

"Who the fuck do you think you are? I make the calls, and I'm telling you, we're hitting him tonight," he growls.

"The table has to vote on it, and they won't today," I assure him. "Your head isn't right, and fuck, it shouldn't be after this. The guys get that, and they aren't gonna let you go on a suicide mission out of rage and grief."

"I have to do something!" he exclaims.

"And we will. But now's not the time, and deep down you know that. You just want something to do to avoid dealing with the fact that you just lost your old lady and your boy. I'm sorry, man, but getting the rest of us killed isn't the way to do that."

"This is all your fucking fault," he says as he presses his index finger into my chest.

"Yeah, it is," I agree, taking responsibility. I'd rather Torin put all the guilt on me rather than take it on his own shoulders. I've been there, and it's a fucking awful place to be. "And I'm so goddamn sorry that it came to this. If I had known..."

"Get the hell away from me," Torin says as he pushes past me and storms out into the hallway.

Before I leave, I go over and say goodbye to Kennedy, leaving a kiss on her forehead. "I'm so sorry, sweetheart," I tell her. "I'll watch over Torin and won't let him do anything stupid," I promise. Then, on the way out, I lay a hand over my nephew's head and assure him the same thing.

CHAPTER TWENTY-FOUR

Sasha

THE *SAVAGE ASYLUM* IS QUIET WHEN EVERYONE RETURNS FROM the hospital. It's hard to forget what happened here with the pieces of crime scene tape still up.

"Jade," Chase says when we walk in and find the auburn-haired woman sitting at the bar in her tan sheriff uniform...and a baby bump that just reminds me of what Torin lost.

"Hey," Jade says as she climbs off the stool with the help of the young, muscular man beside her.

Chase and Jade embrace, then she asks, "How's Torin?"

"Fucking devastated," he tells her. "He's outside, talking to our dad and your mom." Looking down at her belly, he says, "Sorry, but you're probably the last person he wants to see right now."

"God, I know. That's why I didn't come to the hospital. I feel awful," she says. Turning to the guy I now realize is with her, she asks, "Could you go get my coat out of the car, hon? I can try to cover my bump with it."

"Sure," he agrees before giving her a kiss on her cheek.

"This is my husband Knox, by the way," Jade says in introduction. "We had a small, quick ceremony in a church garden a few weeks back."

My eyes widen in surprise since the guy seems tough, like a bad boy from the wrong side of the tracks rather than the husband of a sheriff.

"Don't look so surprised, Sasha," she says to me. "You and Chase don't exactly look like a perfect match either."

"Sorry, I just wasn't expecting that," I tell her. Giving her a hug, I say, "It's good to see you again, Jade. You had braces the last time I saw you."

"Ugh, don't remind me," she says when she pulls away. "I was such a dork in high school."

"I need to see pictures of this," her husband says.

"Her mom has them all, I'm sure. Ask her to see them sometime," Chase says to him.

"I definitely will, thanks," Knox tells him on the way out.

Pulling me close to him, Chase asks his stepsister, "So, what have you found out?"

"Not much," she replies with a sigh. "I know that's not what you want to hear. And if I had to guess, I bet you guys already have a better lead than I do."

"Anyone see the driver?" I ask.

"No. There weren't any witnesses. All we know is that they didn't waste any bullets. They fired just the two shots that didn't miss, nine-millimeter slugs."

The three of us are silent a moment before Jade says, "Chase, please don't do anything stupid. Or let Torin."

"I won't," he agrees. "He needs some time to heal and cool off before he goes out packing heat. I'll find his guns and lock them up."

"That's a start," Jade agrees. "But what happens in a few days or a few weeks? I'm not stupid, Chase. I know you guys are gonna go after whoever is responsible. And I get that. Part of me wants to be right there with you," she says. "But at the same time, bloodshed only leads to more bloodshed. Then it's an endless cycle, and everyone keeps losing. Give me the names. Let me do what I do and help pin this on the person responsible so that no one else has to die."

"You know we can't do that, Jade. That's not who we are," Chase tells her.

Looking to me, Jade says, "Try to talk some sense into my stubborn stepbrother, will you?"

I nod, even though we both know that there's not a damn thing anyone could do to stop the Savage Kings from going after Hector.

"Let me know if you find out anything else," Chase tells her. "We've got three guys on Torin to make sure he stays put, and it's been a helluva day. I don't think I can take much more."

"I get it," Jade says. With one last hug for him and me, she says goodbye. Chase grabs my hand and pulls me downstairs to his room where we both undress and then curl up together under the sheets in his bed.

"I wish I could wake up tomorrow and find out *this* was just a nightmare," he says into my hair as we lay on our sides facing each other.

"Me too," I agree. "I never thought something so awful could happen to someone so good."

"Torin won't recover from this. How could he?" Chase asks.

"I dunno," I reply. "Tomorrow we'll have to start making funeral arrangements."

"Fuck," Chase groans as he pulls me to him tighter. "The punches won't stop coming, neither will these goddamn tears."

"It's okay," I tell him as I rub my hands up and down his bare back, over his tattoo that's identical to the MC's patch.

"I don't want you to think that I'm less of a man now that you've seen me cry," he says softly.

"I don't think that," I assure him as I close my eyes and breathe him in, the way he smells, the way his warmth feels in my arms. I'm so damn happy that I'm here with him. "In fact, it makes me think you're more of a man because you care so much. It's okay to be upset, to cry, to love and to grieve."

"Thanks, sweetheart," he says. "I don't know what I would do without you."

"Me either," I agree. "I just hate that we had to find each other again right when there's a tragedy."

"Torin blames me."

"What?" I exclaim. "He's just upset, sad and angry. You don't believe that, do you?" I ask with concern.

"Well, it is my fault," he says simply. Pulling back enough to look at me, he says, "I set everything into motion, pushing over that first domino when I beat the shit out of one of the Aces. They called Hector, his men pulled Abe and me over, and then from there, it's all on me."

"No, it's not," I disagree. Holding his face in my hands, I tell him, "Your brother doesn't want to admit it, but he's the one responsible. He shouldn't have gotten into the mess with Hector."

"You're right," he agrees. "But the other day, after I killed one of his men, Hector told Torin to hand me over. When he didn't, I guess he decided to take out Kennedy instead to hurt Torin for not giving me up. She died because of me."

"No, baby, don't say that," I tell him as I brush my lips over his and wrap my arms around his neck to hug him. "Hector's responsible. You and Torin may have added fuel to the fire, but he crossed a terrible line."

"I don't know what's gonna happen now," Chase says.

Placing a kiss over my name on his chest, I tell him, "I do. We're gonna get through this together. And when we come out on the other side, we'll probably be a little banged up, but we'll make it because we have each other."

"I love you," he says when he reaches for me and brings my lips to his.

"I love you too," I tell him. Kissing him again, I say, "And that's all we need to know right now."

...

Chase falls asleep pretty fast after we stop talking. He didn't get much sleep last night, and after everything today, he was emotionally exhausted.

For some reason, I can't seem to sleep. I feel all out of sorts, like I need to be doing something for the guys.

I know Chase and I didn't eat any dinner. I bet the other guys haven't either, too stunned and worried about their president to remember to eat.

Slipping out of Chase's arms, I get up and get dressed again.

I'm pretty sure there's a kitchen upstairs back behind the bar. I wonder if they keep any food stocked in it for the brothers.

That's where I head now. The music of the bar sounds muted until I open the door at the top of the stairs. Unlike most nights, the room is pretty quiet; the jukebox turned down lower as if they're afraid the sounds will be offensive to Torin.

Speaking of... "Where's Torin?" I ask Abe, who's nursing a beer at the bar while staring off into the distance.

"He's out back with War and the prospects, shooting at targets."

"Oh," I mutter. That doesn't sound like the best thing for him to be doing.

"They're using silencers," Abe adds, like that makes it all better.

"Okay," I say as I look around the room that's mostly filled with club sluts that are chewing their nails and looking uncomfortable.

"Where are the rest of the guys?" I ask Abe.

"Group ride up the coast," he says.

"You sure they won't try to go south after Hector?" I ask.

"Nah," he replies. Taking a swig of beer, he says, "They won't do anything unless we vote it. Tonight's just about getting a little peace. No better place than the road to do that."

Curious, I ask, "Why aren't you with them?"

He lifts a dark eyebrow as he looks at me, like it's so obvious he doesn't know why I would bother asking. "Because Chase is here."

Placing a hand on his thick arm and squeezing it, I tell him, "You're a good friend, Abe."

Shrugging, he tosses back the rest of the beer and then sets it down on the bar. "I think you meant to say *brother*."

"Right," I agree. "Chase is lucky to have you."

He burps loudly in agreement.

"Now, what are we going to do about them?" I ask as I eye the girls.

"No clue," Abe replies. "They've been swarming around like a hive of restless bees. I told them to go home, but they won't."

"I get it," I say, realizing that they're feeling that same restless energy as I am. "Girls!" I call out to get their attention. "Group meeting in the kitchen."

They're still looking at each other questioningly when I head through the door that leads to the area on the backside of the bar. I was right; it's an enormous kitchen with brand new appliances that look like they've never been used, other than the dishwasher with rows of glasses sitting beside it.

Eventually, two girls trickle in and then three more. Finally, all six are gathered together, arms wrapped around themselves because it's cold back here and they're not wearing many clothes.

"Why are you all just sitting around?" I ask, crossing my arms over my chest.

They exchange looks before a brunette says, "We don't know what to do."

"Yeah, well, me neither," I agree with a sigh. "You want to do something though, right?"

"Yes," most of them agree or nod their heads in agreement.

"We tried to talk to the guys, but none of them wanted us tonight," a blonde speaks up and says.

"They're trying to deal with something they've probably never experienced before," I explain. "Something that's going to send this club into a tailspin before they're finally able to correct it. Give the guys space. But you did the right thing by sticking around. They're gonna need you, whether they'll admit it to you or themselves. Losing someone close makes you want to celebrate life, sometimes in the act that creates it. The men will get there, just be patient," I assure them. "In the meantime, we need to keep them fed."

Going over to the large refrigerator, I pull it open and find it stocked full of beer but no food.

"Who wants to run to the grocery store?" I ask. "We can provide some comfort food until the guys want the other type of comfort."

"I'll go," a brunette offers.

"I can help her," a redhead volunteers.

"Great," I reply. "I'll make you a list of some things for sandwiches tonight and then breakfast tomorrow. Now, does anyone know how to cook anything? All I can do is use the microwave."

A blonde with a bad dye job raises her hand, bless her heart. "I can cook omelettes."

"Awesome. You'll be our omelette girl first thing tomorrow morning. Be here by seven to get started."

She gives an enthusiastic nod of agreement.

"Can anyone make a casserole or lasagna? Something to heat up fast?" I ask.

No one speaks up.

Great, we're a generation that lives on fast food.

"That's okay," I say. "I'll add some frozen ones to the grocery list, and we'll heat them in the oven. How about desserts?"

I get a few takers there and tell them all to bring in their dishes by lunchtime tomorrow, since you can never have enough desserts. Even if the guys say they're not hungry, I bet they'll eat a slice of apple pie.

When everyone has agreed to help out with something, and I've written out the list of everything we'll need from the store, I tell the women to scatter and go do their good deeds. It's better than them staying here all night, not getting any sleep. Who knows when the brothers will be back? Besides, I'm guessing they'll all be like Chase when they do return – just want a bed to pass out in.

Finally feeling like I'm ready for a little sleep myself, I decide to take a peek outside to check on Torin before I go back downstairs.

Pop. Pop. Pop. Pop.

Torin fires his weapon, one quiet shot after another thanks to the silencer, until the slide racks open when his clip empties.

"Give me another," he says to War, who is standing beside him at the ready. On the ground are the two prospects, each of them pressing bullets into additional clips from boxes of bullets.

"You guys need anything?" I ask while Torin reloads. He doesn't even look at me before he cocks the weapon and starts firing again.

"Nah, darlin'. We're fine," War says. The prospects both mime drinking a beer, so I grab four and bring them back, setting them down next to them.

"I'll be down in Chase's room if anyone needs anything," I say before I slip back inside.

Undressing, because I love the feel of Chase's skin against mine, I crawl back under the covers and become the big spoon against his back, throwing an arm over his waist and pressing a few kisses to the bearded skull tattoo on his back. Other than cover my hand on his waist and bring it up to his lips to kiss, Chase doesn't say anything before I finally drift off to sleep.

CHAPTER TWENTY-FIVE

Chase

When I wake up with Sasha in my arms, her backside to the front of my body, I'm happier than I've felt in years. Then, I remember the day before, and I go from feeling joy to fury in seconds.

I'm so fucked in my head that it takes a second to realize that my dick is soft. When was the last time I didn't wake up with morning wood? That's how bad things are. I have a gorgeous woman naked in my bed, and I don't even have the urge to fuck her.

My chest aches too badly with the loss of Kennedy and my nephew that it doesn't ever feel like things will go back to normal in my life.

First things first, we need to sit everyone down and talk things out, make sure no one does anything to make shit worse like I did.

Kissing Sasha's cheek, I roll out of bed; then shower and get dressed.

Sitting down with my phone on the charger, since I forgot to do that yesterday, I type out a text to Sax, asking if Torin's called everyone here. If not, I tell him to do it for me since I want to hold church in an hour.

Then, I get to my feet to go look for my brother.

The door to the chapel is shut when I approach it, so I turn the knob and walk inside, assuming this is where I'll find Torin.

And I do.

I wasn't expecting to walk in and find him with his big ass Army knife out taking it to his cut.

"What the fuck are you doing?" I ask him.

"I can't do this," he says without looking over at me.

"Do what?" I ask as I walk up and see that he's already removed half the thread for the president flash on the front.

"She trusted me," Torin says. "To protect her, to keep her and the baby safe. And I betrayed her."

"What? No, man. This isn't on you."

Stabbing the knife's point into the wooden table, he says, "I couldn't take care of my old lady or my boy. How the fuck can I be responsible for this club?"

"Look, I can't even imagine how hard this is for you right now," I start. "But the club needs you in charge. Who else is gonna do it, if not you?" I ask.

He turns around and holds out the president patch to me. "You."

"Hell no," I tell him, refusing to accept it. "Why would you think I can lead? You blame me for all this shit, remember?"

When I don't take the patch, he lays it on the table and then picks up his cut to put it back on, still stained with Kennedy's blood.

"This is on me," Torin says. "It's all on me. I'm sorry I said that to you yesterday. I was just angry and wanted to blame someone else."

"Then blame fucking Hector!" I exclaim.

"If I hadn't fucked up, he wouldn't have had anything to blackmail me with," Torin replies. "Now that she's gone, it doesn't matter anymore. He's a goddamn idiot for removing the one reason I was paying him. The one reason I didn't just kill him."

"Yeah, he is," I agree, assuming that Torin was only paying

Hector off to prevent Kennedy from finding out what he did. "*We're* gonna kill him," I promise. "You can't do it alone."

"I won't," he agrees. "I've got funeral plans and shit to make. I know you won't let me down. When you say it's time, it's time. That's your call now. Just give me a few days," he says before he starts to walk out the door.

"Torin!" I yell to stop him. His feet pause, his shoulders hunched like they're carrying the weight of the fucking world, but he doesn't turn around. "We have church in less than an hour. Everyone's on their way in."

"Good," he says. "You're in charge, and you've got my proxy. Whatever you decide."

"Torin!" I call out again, but this time he doesn't stop. He's down the hall and gone.

Jogging back to my room, I grab my cell phone and call War.

"I'm up here with him," he answers, knowing why I'm calling.

"Good. I'll find you after we meet," I tell him, figuring he probably needs to get home to check on his kid and get some sleep.

After I hang up, I realize that I should've called him out in the hallway because I woke up Sasha.

"Hey," she says as she sits up in bed to look at me, her hair a tangled mess. She's so fucking beautiful it hurts. "You hungry?" she asks.

"No," I reply automatically before adding, "But I probably need to eat something before my stomach starts fucking eating itself."

"Head upstairs. The girls should have breakfast ready. I'll come help as soon as I get a shower," she says.

"Okay," I agree. "I've got a meeting in about half an hour."

"Good," she says as she climbs out of bed and comes over to hug me. "We'll make sure the guys all eat something too."

"We?" I ask as I hold her in my arms, not ready to let her go yet.

"I got the girls to pitch in on feeding you all for the next few days."

"You did, huh?" I ask with a small smile, impressed that she's not only getting along with the club sluts but putting them to work. I'll be even more surprised if they actually listen to her. Those girls don't like other women telling them what to do, especially one that's sleeping with the same bastard they used to fool around with.

"They just wanted to do something too," Sasha says. "Everyone's worried about you guys. How's Torin this morning?"

"Fucked up," I grumble. "We'll talk about all that later, okay, sweetheart?"

"Yeah," she agrees. Giving me a quick kiss on the lips, she says, "I love you."

"Love you, too," I reply.

...

Sasha

AFTER I GET a quick shower and dry my hair, I head upstairs. I'm so glad to see the bar full of men eating rather than drinking their emotions this early in the morning. The club girls came through.

"Sasha?"

I turn at the sound of my name and find... an older version of Chase – his father. His reddish-blond hair is nearly white after ten years but he still looks the same, tall and handsome, just like his sons.

"Hi, Mr. Fury," I say before I go up to him and hug him. I didn't get a chance to speak to him last night.

"Well, I'll be," he says as he leans back, holding me by my upper arms to look at me again. "What are you doing here, doll?"

"I guess Chase hasn't told you with everything going on," I reply. "We're back together."

"That's wonderful!" his father says before hugging me once more. "It's so good to see you again. Especially now."

"I'm so sorry for your loss," I tell him.

"Thank you, doll," he says when he releases me. "Kennedy was just an angel on earth. I don't know what we'll do without her. I don't know what Torin will do..." he starts before he gets choked up. Pulling out a handkerchief from his button down's pocket, he blows his nose and apologizes. "Sorry, sorry. Keeps sneaking up on me."

"I understand," I tell him, reaching up to squeeze his shoulder. "How's Mrs. Fury? Is she here?"

"Yes, she's well, thanks for asking. She's in the kitchen," he replies. "I know she'll be so glad to see you too. We may have lost one sweet daughter-in-law, but at least we gained another."

"Thank you," I tell him. "I wish I would've been able to get to know Kennedy better. She seemed like such a wonderful woman."

"She was," he agrees. "And Torin was damn lucky she put up with him."

"Dad," Chase calls out before he comes over and wraps his father in a long embrace. "Glad you made it back over here again today. Torin just left..."

"How are you doing, son? Did you get any sleep last night?" Mr. Fury asks.

"Yeah, a little," Chase answers. "It's been tough."

"We're here if you need anything. Just ask," his father says to him. "And why didn't you tell me that you were back with Miss Sasha, huh?"

"I was meaning to, but things have been crazy," Chase replies.

"I'm happy for you two. We needed some good news right now. So, tell me," he starts before putting one arm around Chase's shoulders and the other around mine. "When's the wedding?"

"Don't rush us, old man," Chase tells his dad before he slips away from his arm. "And I hate to run, but we've got some business to take care of downstairs."

"Right, sure," his father says. "You boys be careful."

"We will," Chase agrees. Giving me a quick kiss, he says, "I'll see you in a few."

"Okay," I agree before he tips his head toward the basement door and all the men get up and follow.

After they're gone, his dad continues to stare off silently in the direction they went. Eventually he says, "Chase is in charge."

"What?" I ask.

"Torin's unable to lead, so it falls on Chase's shoulders. He's the man in charge now," he explains.

"Really? You think so?" I ask. "Chase hasn't mentioned it."

"My youngest son isn't cut out to run things. He'll need you to help him stay level," Mr. Fury tells me. "Take care of my boy."

"I will," I agree, even though I'm starting to worry even more about what these changes in the club mean for Chase and me.

...

Chase

I TAKE my usual seat at the table, leaving Torin's chair at the head of the table empty. It still belongs to him, and I know he will be back. In the meantime, I guess that means I'm the one who will be calling the shots.

And fuck me, but I'm already feeling the pressure of everyone's eyes on me, like they know I'm not equal to the load I'm about to try and lift.

Picking up the president flash from the table, I rub it between my fingers, and then tell the group, "Given what happened yesterday, Torin has decided to step down."

There are murmurs around the table.

"I'm not taking over for him. I won't even take his seat, but I will be the club's leader until he's able to come back," I tell them. Lifting my eyes to look at every single man one at a time, I give them the cold, hard truth. "Over the next few days, weeks, hell, maybe even months, this club is going to be in an all-out war with Hector Cruz. The fucker's apparently overlooked the word *Savage* in our goddamn names. Otherwise, he wouldn't have been stupid enough to kill one of our old ladies on our fucking turf. He has to pay for what he did. The reasons why the feud with him started don't matter anymore. I accept responsibility for the role I played, but if he wanted to kill someone, it should've been me, not an innocent woman and her unborn child." Taking a deep breath, I add, "I want every single one of you to think carefully from now until the funeral. We always talk about loyalty and brotherhood, but now it's time to step up and back those words up with action. Dig deep and decide if you're ready to kill for this MC and die for your brothers. Going forward, both those things aren't possibilities; they're certainties."

Some of the guys slap their palms on the table over and over again as a show of their support and agreement.

"We'll meet again the night of the funeral, and I only want to see men who are ready for war at this table."

More hands join in slapping the table.

"I don't need the time to think. Count me in," Abe says from my left.

"I'm in," Sax agrees from the other side of him.

"Me too," Dalton adds.

"I can't wait to kill some fucking rat bastards," Miles says.

"Let's do this," Gabe agrees. "For Kennedy."

"For Kennedy," Reece agrees.

"For Torin and Kennedy," Cooper speaks up as the table comes back around to him, sitting next to War's empty chair.

"I know War and Torin are in," I tell him. "The other chapters will be coming into town from across the country for the funeral.

We'll see who wants to join us. If nothing else, we could use the other members to keep the police out while we hit the motherfucker."

"Agreed," the guys say.

Reaching for the gavel, the wooden handle feels all wrong in my hand. Still, I slam it down, calling an end to our meeting.

"You've got this, brother," Abe says when I get to my feet, and he stands up to clasp me on the back.

"We'll see," I tell him. "Now, I have to call the funeral home and see when I can bring Torin in to make arrangements," I grumble. "It's so fucking wrong. Even seeing her in the hospital and saying goodbye, I can't believe she's gone."

"Fuck, me either," Abe replies. "I couldn't sleep last night, kept seeing that damn scene outside in the parking lot over and over again. Kennedy bleeding and none of us being able to do a goddamn thing to stop it."

"I hate you had to witness that," I tell him.

"I'm pretty sure that shit is gonna haunt me for the rest of my life," he says with a shake of his head.

"You need something to help you sleep? My dad or Sasha can probably hook you up with some pills," I tell Abe.

"Nah, man. I'm gonna go find some tits to drown myself in for a little while, see if that helps."

"Good luck," I tell him, thinking he's a lucky bastard.

I'd rather be losing myself in Sasha right now, but my head's not in it, and I've got too much shit to do. I need to find my brother and take him to pick out a casket.

Going back to my room, I pull my phone off the charger and then call War.

"Yeah?" he asks, sounding dead tired.

"Where are you?" I ask.

"Torin's house."

"Really?" I ask, surprised he'd want to go back there so soon.

"Or I guess I should've said what's left of it," War adds.

"Fuck," I grumble as I scrub my hand down my face. "How bad is it?"

"It's still standing," he answers. "I tried to talk him out of it, told him that in a few days he would regret it, but he wouldn't listen. I figured he needs the physical exertion."

"Has he slept any?" I ask.

"No. He was up shooting rounds out back until we ran out of ammo. He's gonna crash soon, and hard."

"I know," I agree. "I'm on my way over so that you can go home and rest."

"Appreciate it. I really wanna hug my kid, you know?"

"Yeah, man, I get it," I tell him. "See you in a few."

I start to find Sasha before I leave the bar, but for some reason that I can't put my finger on, seeing her right now is just too fucking hard. Probably because I can't stop thinking that it could've been her in that hospital bed and that if she stays with me, one of these days it likely will be.

CHAPTER TWENTY-SIX

Sasha

"So, you and Chase went out in high school?" one of the club girls asks while I'm washing dishes and she's rinsing and drying. Cynthia, I believe is her name.

"Yeah, we did," I reply with a smile as I scrub the coffee pot. "We dated a little over six months."

"What happened? Why did you split up?" she asks. "It must have been serious if he got your name inked on his chest."

"We had a wreck one night when we were out on his bike, the night he got that ink," I admit to her. "I was hurt pretty bad, had to have a few surgeries. After all these years, I thought he didn't want to see me, but it turns out my parents told him I blamed him and didn't want to see him. Which were flat out lies. They ruined what we had with just a few words..."

"So that's why he doesn't let anyone on the back of his bike," she says while she rinses out the coffee pot to get the suds out.

"He doesn't?"

"Nope."

"Ever?" I ask as I hand her a sudsy coffee mug.

"No. He rides alone, always has since I've been coming around. The other girls that have been here longer say that it's a no-go. And that he only likes blondes, so not to waste my time."

"Oh really?" I reply.

"Yeah. But Abe likes redheads, so it's all good," she says with a grin.

"So I've heard," I say as I grab the next dish, a frying pan to scrub. "He's a good guy, right?" I ask.

"Who? Abe? Oh, yeah, he's great. He's the only one who actually likes to cuddle afterward."

"Really? That's surprising. Although, he does look like a big bear."

"Yeah, he's a big ole teddy bear," Cynthia agrees with a grin.

"Have you, you know, been with the other guys?" I ask curiously.

"Not all of them. Never Torin or Chase, of course; but I've been with Sax and Miles a few times."

"Wow," I mutter. "And you don't mind them...sharing you?"

"God, no," she replies without hesitation. "It's no different than dating a few different men. Just so happens the men I date know each other."

"Yeah, but don't you eventually want more?" I ask.

"Well, yeah," she says. "That's why I sleep with them. Hopefully one will keep me in his bed and never let me go."

Poor girl. I don't want to bust her bubble, but I don't think it works like that with these guys.

"What if none of them ever want to settle down with you?" I ask.

"Then I'll have had enough great sex to last me the rest of my life."

Can't disagree with that since Chase is a much better lover than the other men I've been with. But that's not the only reason I love him. He's sweet and hard headed and loyal. Chase looks at me like I'm the only woman in the world and like he would do anything under the sun for me. What woman doesn't want that?

...

Chase

As soon as I pull my bike into Torin's driveway, War comes out the side door and down the stairs, probably having heard my muffler a mile back.

"I love your brother, but he's all yours now," War says as he passes me and climbs on his ride.

"Thanks, man," I say before he cranks it up.

The fact that War, my brother's best friend, was so ready to leave means it must be bad.

Holden and Maddox both look pitiful as they each sit on different steps out front, leaning their heads against the rails. "You guys can go home and get some rest," I tell them. "We'll take Torin's SUV when we leave, and I'll call you tonight when I need you back on him."

"Yes, sir," they both murmur before they trudge down the steps and ride off in the MC's van.

Walking into Torin and Kennedy's home, knowing how happy it was a few days ago and that it'll never be that way again is agonizing. Even though I was a miserable sack of shit without Sasha these last few years, it was nice to know that my brother had someone he loved and who loved him back just as much. Now, he's lost everything that mattered to him, other than the MC, which he's trying to pull away from.

I don't hear anything as I step into the house, so I call out, "Torin?"

He doesn't answer. I walk past each room until I finally find him. He's sitting on the floor in the nursery. His back is resting against the crib, and he's holding one of the black and white sonograms of the baby that Kennedy framed.

Looking up at me through glassy, red-rimmed eyes with bags underneath that are as big as carry-on luggage, Torin says, "I didn't want to be a father. The day Kennedy told me she was pregnant, I was shocked and scared. I was a complete asshole."

"That's probably the same thing every man experiences when he's told that news," I assure him.

"I should've been excited. I was married to the most incredible woman in the world, and my first reaction was to want to bail."

"You didn't, though," I point out.

"I know why. The first time I went to the doctor with Kennedy and saw the baby on the screen, I fell in love with it. Didn't know if it was a boy or girl, and I didn't care. It was ours."

"Yeah, I know," I agree. "I'm sorry, Torin."

"I was a horrible husband. If Kennedy knew..."

"You weren't a horrible husband. And Kennedy knew you loved her. She loved you too, more than anything."

"And look how that ended for her," he grumbles before he throws the picture against the wall, making me wince when it shatters. There's something horrible about the sound of glass breaking; maybe it's because you know, once it's broken, you can never put the shards back together. They'll cut you and make you bleed, but they won't glue back into one piece again.

It reminds me of the night I broke into Sasha's house and scared her. I cringed the same way when I heard the wine bottle break, because I was worried she would hurt herself and it would be my fault. It is always my fault when she gets hurt.

"The, um, the funeral home said that you could come by any time today," I tell Torin, who nods from his seat. "We can go now, or you can try to get some sleep and we can go later."

"I don't want to go," he replies.

"You wanna wait until tomorrow?" I ask. "I know it sucks, but we need to make all the arrangements. The other charters are calling, wanting to know..."

"No, I mean I don't want to make the arrangements."

Fuck.

"Don't check out on me, man," I tell him. "I can help you, but I can't do it all myself."

Torin doesn't respond for a while before he says, "If I could go back in time, I'd call off our wedding..."

"No, you wouldn't," I tell him on a heavy exhale.

"Yes, I would've. I almost did. That morning, there was this gnawing in my gut telling me to bail, to leave because I didn't deserve her after what I did. I should've listened. I just couldn't stand the thought of her hating me for not showing up at the altar, you know? And she would have. God, she would've killed me if I had bailed."

"If you had bailed, you wouldn't have had the time you did with her," I point out.

"I'd rather have nothing with her than this," he says. "This empty fucking house that I didn't spend enough time with her in. And this empty fucking hole inside of me that hurts with every fucking breath I try and take."

Going over, I grab his arm and try to pull him to his feet. "Come on," I say, unable to listen to anything else. It's too raw and too painful to hear.

"Leave me the fuck alone," he growls.

"No. Get the fuck up. We're going to make arrangements, and then you're gonna get some sleep, even if I have to knock you out to make it happen."

Finally, he stops fighting against me and lets me pull him to his feet.

"I wish everyone would leave me the hell alone," he says.

"Come with me to the funeral home, and then I'll take you to the farmhouse. No one will be able to find you or talk to you, and you won't be surrounded by all of this," I say as I gesture around the room with my arms.

This house isn't good for Torin. There are too many memories. He's suffocating in them here. So tonight, once the tough part is over, I'll take him to the empty house we grew up in before he ever met Kennedy.

And when he's not looking, I'll crush some sleeping pills up and put them in his drink. If he doesn't get some sleep soon, I'm afraid he's gonna lose his goddamn mind.

CHAPTER TWENTY-SEVEN

Sasha

"Sorry to interrupt, but have you seen Chase?" I ask Abe after I look all over the bar and downstairs for him. That's why I hated to do it, but I knocked on Abe's door and interrupted him getting 'consoled' by Cynthia.

"He slipped out on me earlier," Abe tells me, holding a towel around his waist.

"Well, where did he go?" I ask.

"Dunno. I sent him a text, but he didn't respond," he says. "Figured he didn't want me tagging along."

"He didn't answer my texts either," I say in concern. "What about his dad? Do you have his number?"

"Ah, yeah. Hang on." He shuts the door and then returns a minute later with his phone in his hand and calls out Mr. Fury's number.

"Thanks, and sorry again for bothering you," I tell Abe as I walk off, trying to call Chase's dad.

"Hello?" he answers.

"Mr. Fury, hi, it's Sasha," I say.

"Oh, hi, Sasha."

"Sorry to call you, but I was wondering if you've seen Chase."

"Oh, yeah," he replies. "We just left him and Torin at the funeral home. They were finishing up the paperwork."

"Oh," I mutter, glad to know where he is but wondering why he didn't tell me he was leaving, or ask me to go with him. Maybe he thought it would be best to go alone with Torin and his dad.

"Do you know if they're coming back here to the clubhouse?" I ask.

"Nah, I think Chase was gonna take Torin to our old house and stay there with him so he can rest. Torin asked that everyone give him a little time alone."

"Right, of course," I say in understanding. "Then I'll just stay here and wait for Chase to call."

"Sounds good, doll. Take care of yourself," Mr. Fury tells me.

"You too," I say before I end the call.

Earlier I was worried that Chase was keeping things from me, and now he up and left without telling me. I don't mind that he's with Torin; I just would've liked to know so I wouldn't worry about him. Hector is obviously crazy, and Chase could be in danger.

I just hope that everything is okay with us and that I'm over-reacting.

The problem is that I can't help but think that Chase is pulling away from me because he's still worried about me getting hurt. Does he think that what happened to Kennedy could happen to me? Of course, it could, but that doesn't mean it will.

I love Chase enough to stay with him even knowing all the risks associated with him being in the MC.

The question is, does he love me enough to handle me being a part of his outlaw life?

...

Chase

When we got to the farmhouse, Torin finally asked for something to drink. That's when I found some Benadryl, chopped it up and put it in his beer bottle.

I feel bad for drugging my brother, but he needs to take a few hours off from destroying shit and finally get some rest.

At least he didn't break anything at the funeral home before I got him out of there.

Now he's passed out on the sofa, snoring, and I feel like I've been run over by a goddamn bulldozer.

When I pull out my phone, I notice several texts from Sasha and Abe. Since my battery is low, I message Abe back that I'm crashing at the farmhouse and I'll see him tomorrow. Then, I step out on the front porch to call Sasha.

"Chase?" she answers.

"Hey, sweetheart," I say as I lean my forearms on the railing.

"How's everything going?" she asks.

"I finally got Torin to sleep after we took care of all the arrangements. Hopefully, he'll sleep a few hours and I can too."

"Yeah, good," she says, followed by silence.

"I wish you were here," I tell her.

"Do you want me to see if someone can give me a ride over?" she asks.

Thinking about her on the back of any of my brothers' bikes is a big fucking hell no.

"No, sweetheart, just get some rest, and I'll see you tomorrow. Torin just needed someplace to get away from it all, you know?"

"Yeah, sure," Sasha agrees.

"Sleep in tomorrow," I tell her. "I'll get the prospects over here early in the morning after they get some rest, then I'll come curl up in bed with you."

"Can't wait," she says. "I love you."

"Love you too," I reply before ending the call.

And fuck, I do love her so goddamn much it scares me.

For ten years I thought that being with Sasha again was what I wanted more than anything, but now I don't know what the hell I was thinking. She was safe without me in her life and doing pretty damn good. Now, she's worried that she could lose her job in television if she's with me. But more importantly, if we're together, she could lose a lot more than her career.

I worried myself to death about her when we weren't together; but now that she's back in my life, I worry even more.

Sasha loves me, and I know she loves danger, but neither of those things are good for her.

When we hit Hector back, we'll be in a bloody feud that could last weeks or longer. I don't want Sasha to get caught up in the middle of that shit.

So maybe the best thing I can do for her is to give her up, even if just the thought of losing her is agonizing.

CHAPTER TWENTY-EIGHT

Sasha

EARLY THIS MORNING CHASE SNUCK INTO BED WITHOUT A word. After he wrapped his arms around me, he fell fast asleep. Even though he's here, in the same room with me, I can't help but feel that he's actually miles away.

Unable to lie in bed any longer, I get up and head upstairs to start helping with breakfast. The guys have been hanging around the bar more. Last night it was a full house, yet the crowd was still quiet as if they were afraid that talking or laughing would be disrespectful to their president.

Throughout the day, I hear the roar of bikes as more and more Savage Kings come into town from up and down the east coast. I welcome each one and ask if they're hungry or need me to find them someplace to stay. The hotel is booked out completely, but some of the guys have offered to share their rooms with double beds, if needed. I put members wherever I can, squeeze them in, except for the farmhouse.

I read online that the funeral is at eleven, graveside only to accommodate all of the guests. The fact that Chase didn't even tell me that much information makes me a little sad.

By the time Chase wakes up around noon, we have a full house at the *Savage Asylum.* The place is growing rowdier too, which you would expect when you cram about two hundred Kings into one bar.

"Hey, sweetheart," Chase says when he comes up to me at the bar. I've been chatting with a few members, hearing their crazy road and clubhouse stories.

"Hi, baby," I say when he gives me a quick kiss on the lips. Before I can say anything else, Chase is swamped with well-wishers coming to pay their respects. Torin is still hiding out at the farmhouse, as far as I know; and the bar isn't exactly the type of place for their parents to hang out for long periods of time.

If I remember correctly, Chase's dad never really approved of the MC. His brother, Chase and Torin's uncle, Deacon Fury, was the president when the boys were growing up. The guys looked up to him and wanted to be like their cool, Harley-riding uncle. Despite their dad's attempts to sway them in any other direction, Chase wouldn't have it. As soon as he turned eighteen, he started prospecting with Deacon as his mentor. Then, when Torin returned from the military, I guess he fell into the club pretty hard if he was able to be elected president within a few years.

When I get Chase alone for a minute, I ask him, hoping he'll open up to me.

"How did Torin become president before you?" I ask.

"What? Why do you want to know about that?"

"Just curious. You patched in first."

"I never wanted the gavel," he replies with a shrug. "And Torin had been running things for Deacon when he started getting sick. By the time the lung cancer took him, Torin was handling the entire business side of things, so he was the better choice. And he wanted to be in charge."

"Are you in charge now?" I ask, since he hasn't talked to me about it.

"Just filling in for Torin until he's ready," he says.

"So you are?"

"Technically, I guess. Why all the questions?" he says as he pulls back.

"You haven't said much over the last few days. Is everything okay? Are we okay?"

"Yeah, baby, we're great," Chase answers, using a different term of endearment. He's always called me sweetheart since our first date.

There's no time to question him further, because the door opens and in walks a beautiful brunette in a bright yellow sundress, looking almost as out of place as I did the first time I came into the bar. And if she didn't draw everyone's eyes and attention, the two tall men who come in behind her would.

"Hi," the girl says to the silent room over the rock song playing softly on the jukebox. And for some reason, not only does she look oddly familiar, even though I don't think I've ever seen her before, the men are definitely recognizable. They're professional football players from the Wilmington Wildcats. "I'm, ah, looking for Torin Fury," she says.

"He's not here," Chase speaks up and says as he steps toward her. "Is there something I can help you with?"

"I got a call from him yesterday morning about my, ah, my sister..."

Her eyes tear up; and as if on cue, both men reach forward to comfort her.

"You're Kelsey, Kennedy's sister?" Chase asks in understanding.

She nods as her chin trembles.

"Let's go outside to talk," Chase suggests to her, and I get up to follow them.

...

Chase

Wow. Kennedy's sister looks so much like her that it's eerie. And the two big guys escorting her I frequently see on Sundays, catching touchdowns for the Wildcats.

Once we're outside where there aren't hundreds of eyes on us, I hold out my hand and say, "I'm Chase, Torin's brother."

"Nice to meet you," Kelsey replies. "I wish we all could've met sooner; but once Kennedy ran off with your MC, she stopped answering my calls. I got one message from her about three years ago saying she was safe and wasn't coming home. That was it until...until Torin called from her phone yesterday morning."

"I'm so damn sorry you had to find out that way," I tell her.

"What happened?" she asks, crossing her arms over her chest.

"Drive-by shooting," I explain. "We're looking into it and *will* find who did this."

"How was she, before...before this happened?" Kelsey asks, her voice trembling with emotion. One of the football players pulls her to his side, and the other takes her hand, making me think the three of them are all together. To each their own.

"Kennedy was great," I tell her honestly. "She was happy, excited to become a mother..."

"I, um, I read about that this morning and couldn't believe it. There was so much of her life that I missed, and now I'll never know why because she's gone." The blond man I recognize now as Cameron Hines wraps Kelsey in a hug while she cries against him.

"She was just trying to keep you safe," Sasha speaks up and says from just behind me. I didn't even know that she came outside with us. She reaches for my hand, weaving her fingers through mine as she gives me a small smile. "The MC is dangerous to associate with. Kennedy knew that from the beginning, but it was the life she chose when she married Torin."

"She was her sister, though," Nixon Lopez, the dark-haired man with tattoos, says. "Kelsey lives almost two hours away. She wouldn't have been in any danger by talking to her sister on the phone."

"Talking on the phone would have only made Kennedy want to see her in person, which could've put her at risk. It's fucked up but true," I tell him. "That's why most of us don't have old ladies. Pushing the people you love away is the only way to make sure that you don't lose them the way we lost Kennedy. Since he lost her, Torin's blamed himself for not calling off the wedding. If Kennedy had stayed at home with your family, she would still be alive."

"It wasn't like Torin kidnapped her and forced Kennedy to be his wife," Sasha argues. "She loved him enough to take the chance."

"And now we can't ask her if she regrets it, can we?" I snap at her.

"She wouldn't," Sasha whispers.

Unable to even look at her beautiful face right now, I turn back to Kelsey and her men and say, "I'm so fucking sorry you lost your sister, and I wish I had answers for you. Hell, I wish I could go back in time to the night she met Torin when she was waitressing at that little BBQ joint and tell her to not leave with him."

"She left with him the night they met?" Kelsey asks as she turns back to face me.

"Yeah," I reply. "We were just passing through Wilmington on a run and stopped to eat lunch. The second Torin saw her, he told the rest of us to go on home because he wasn't leaving until he got a chance to talk to her. Guess she liked whatever he said, because she stayed here that night and never left again. She even put up with my brother when he would fuck up and be an idiot."

"I missed her," Kelsey says with a sniffle. "My mom and dad wouldn't even come up here for the funeral because they blame the MC. I blamed Kennedy. I loved her enough that I could've handled the risks. She should've known that."

"I'm sure she did," I tell her. "That's why she decided for you.

Shit around here is volatile. I'd hate for you three to get caught up in this mess."

"We're staying for the funeral," Kelsey says, showing the same stubbornness as her sister.

"I figured as much," I tell her with a smirk. "I'll let Torin know that you're here, and we'll be sure to save you seats at the front tomorrow."

"I appreciate that," the dark-haired guy says, holding out his hand to me. "I'm Nix, by the way."

"Yeah, Nixon Lopez and Cameron Hines. I recognized you," I tell him as I shake his hand and then Cameron's. "I hate we had to meet under these circumstances. But as you can see from the bar full of men in leather, we all loved Kennedy. She didn't deserve what happened to her, and I promise we'll avenge her and the baby's deaths."

With a nod, Kelsey says, "We'll see you tomorrow," and then her and the men walk off toward their car.

"You're not pushing me away out of fear," Sasha says from beside me. Grabbing the collar of my cut to make me face her, she says, "Chase *Franklin* Fury, are you listening to me?"

I glance around to make sure no one is around before I warn her. "Woman, if you ever use my middle name again in public, I'll spank your ass raw."

Watching her lips, I know what she's gonna say probably before she does. More importantly, my cock twitches with anticipation.

"*Franklin.*"

When I scoop her up in a fireman's carry, she shrieks and then laughs as I carry her back through the bar. We're greeted with whistles and cheers from the crowd before I take her down the stairs to my room and toss her on the center of the bed.

I follow her down, attacking her mouth furiously. I hate how hard-headed she is, but love it at the same time. I'm a selfish bastard, because I need her in my life even though I know I shouldn't condemn her to this type of lifestyle. Soon. *I'll let her go soon,* I promise myself as I tear her shirt and shorts off.

"This week is the first time I've worn shorts in public," Sasha admits, making me freeze. "I was embarrassed for anyone to see my scar at the station or on television, but here? I know that the people upstairs won't judge me. They all have scars, some you can see and some you can't, so they don't make me feel bad about it." Reaching down, she rubs her fingers over the long, thick scar. "This place is like home to me, not just because of you."

"We're going to kill Hector and everyone associated with him," I warn her.

Her fingers stroke along my jaw and down to my beard before she says, "I know that."

"And you're okay being with a murderer?"

"Yes," she answers without hesitation. She takes off my cut and pulls my shirt over my head. "I already knew that, remember?"

"I'm not gonna change. I know women think they can fix men or what the fuck ever, but this is me, and no matter how much I love you, I won't leave the MC."

"Yeah, I know that too," Sasha says. Her fingers pop the button on my jeans and slide the zipper down. Reaching inside the open flap, she fists my cock and gives it a hard stroke. "Now stop trying to think of ways to scare me off and fuck me already. Didn't you say something about some spanking?"

"Fuck, yes," I tell her. Grabbing her waist, I flip her over to her stomach and then peel her panties down just under her ass cheeks so that my palm can smack one side.

"Oh, God," Sasha moans as the entire length of her body jerks off the mattress.

I slap the other side of her ass hard, getting the same reaction before I band an arm around her stomach to raise her up to her knees. Then, I spread her legs apart to swat at her pussy.

"Ahh, yes!" Sasha cries out, but it's muted with her face buried in the sheets. "Don't stop," she begs with her ass in the air, squirming in search of my hand that I pulled away. But I don't give her my hand again. Instead, I lean forward and lick her slit from the front all the way to the back where my tongue runs circles around her puckered hole.

"Oh, god, Chase!" she moans as her hips rock, wanting me to lick her on her needy little clit instead. I bury my face in her pussy to give her what she wants until Sasha nearly screams down the walls when she comes on my face. No matter how many times I soap it up, I bet I'll smell her scent in my beard for fucking days.

Still kneeling behind her, I keep an arm around her waist to lift her hips and line my cock up with her slick entrance.

"Fuck!" Sasha and I both shout as I plunge into her depths, not stopping until I'm all the way home. Nothing should feel as good as her body surrounding my cock with its tight, comforting warmth. I hate how I crave being inside of her, with her, but I'm an addict and I can't give her up no matter how hard I try.

My emotions show with every pump of my hips, the tightening of her hair in my fist while I fuck Sasha with more force than I ever have. I'd be worried I'm hurting her if not for her chanting her enthusiastic agreement and praise to the good lord above.

"Yes! Oh, God! Oh, God, yes! Don't stop! So close! I need...I need...*Oh!Oh!Ohhh!*"

Sasha comes for an eternity, clenching and releasing around me for so long, milking my release from me like it's the only thing her body was put on this earth to do.

With one hand holding some of my weight off of her so that I don't crush her ribs, I collapse down onto her back. I know I need to get off of her so that she can breathe, but I love the way she feels being pinned underneath me too much to move just yet. Right now, for this second, she's safe, and nothing can hurt her with me protecting her this way.

"Chase?" Sasha asks.

"Yeah, sweetheart?" I ask.

"Do you feel...any...better now?" she asks between pants.

"Yes," I reply even though I know the blissful state will only last a few more seconds before reality comes crashing down on my head.

"Good," she replies. "You've never...fucked me...like that before."

"I know," I agree with a cringe.

"It was...fucking incredible," she replies, making me grin. "Let's do it again sometime."

I finally make myself roll off of her, leaving her vulnerable to the world again.

"Are you angry with me?" Sasha asks as she curls up to my side and runs her fingertips over the cursive letters spelling out her name.

"No," I tell her, and truly I'm not. I could never be angry with her. I'm angry at myself for being so weak and selfish that I can't live without her.

"You wish that I had stayed in my own little world, though," she states because she knows me so well.

"Sometimes I wonder if I made a mistake coming to your house the other night," I tell her honestly. "I don't want to look back on that night with regret like Torin, thinking of the day he wishes he wouldn't have married Kennedy."

"Hey, just because that horrible tragedy happened to them, doesn't mean it will happen to us," Sasha says, raising up on her elbows to look down at me. "Maybe the worst thing that will happen to us was ten years ago when we both nearly died on the highway because of a drunk driver. It could be all uphill from there."

"Every hill peaks eventually; and the bigger the hill, the steeper the plummet back down," I mutter.

"That's not true. It's just the fear and worry talking," she says. "And I get it, Chase. It's gonna take everyone some time before they can start to recover from the loss of Kennedy. But it doesn't mean that you have to stop living or being with someone you love to avoid heartbreak. Don't you understand that I worry about you too?"

"I'm an outlaw, baby. You'd be stupid not to worry about me," I point out.

"No, I worry about you because I love you. If you were a traveling salesman or an accountant working in a high-rise, I would still worry. That's the flip side to loving people. You care enough to think about losing them and want to avoid it at all costs."

"But I'm not a salesman or an accountant. Their old ladies don't have to worry about retaliation landing on their doorstep if a business deal goes bad."

"True," Sasha agrees. "But those old ladies must be bored out of their fucking minds with their lame ass husbands."

"Wouldn't you rather have a life to live with a boring husband than one that gets cut short too soon because of the bad boy's lifestyle?"

Sitting up in bed, Sasha distracts me with her naked swaying breasts before she asks, "Do you not know me at all? You and I aren't that different. The reason you joined the MC as soon as you turned eighteen was because you looked up to your uncle and wanted the excitement he had in his life rather than the calm one your father has, right?"

I consider that for a moment, thinking back to the reasons I joined the MC. I missed my brother. And I didn't have many friends because I was an asshole who could barely keep from flunking out of high school before I finally dropped out after our wreck. The MC offered me a place I felt like I belonged when I didn't fit in anywhere else.

"My uncle was a bad ass, and I liked the idea of the brotherhood," I admit.

"And you didn't want a boring life..."

"And I didn't want a boring life or a boring wife," I stubbornly admit, pulling her back down on my chest. Thinking about the camaraderie of the MC reminds me of our group ride to the cemetery. Even though I'm scared shitless of putting her on the back of my bike, I want her arms around me on a day like the one coming up. That's why I ask Sasha, "Will you ride with me tomorrow to the funeral?"

"Of course," she answers right away.

"I mean on my bike," I clarify.

"Again, the answer is, of course, Chase. I've been dying to ride with you again."

"Don't use that word," I warn her.

"Sorry," she says with a cringe. "I would love to ride with you tomorrow, and for the rest of my life, however long or short that may be. I will *never* have any regrets when it comes to being with you."

"You say that now..." I start.

"And I'll say it until the day I die," Sasha assures me. "Will you ever regret joining the MC?"

"Hell no," I answer without even needing to think about it.

With a pat on my chest, she says, "That's exactly how I feel about you, baby. My only regret is that we spent ten lonely years apart. Oh, and that you never took me to our senior prom. I would've loved to have seen you just once in a tux, dancing with me. That's it, though, the *only* regrets I'll ever have when it comes to you. So it's time for you to quit fighting it and accept the fact that I'm your old lady and I'm not going anywhere."

CHAPTER TWENTY-NINE

Sasha

TODAY WILL GO DOWN AS ONE OF THE MOST EMOTIONAL OF MY life, which tells you just how powerful a presence Kennedy was in this town and to the MC.

"I can't believe I'm doing this," Chase says as he stands in front of me wearing his jeans and cut with a helmet in his hands. "Are you sure, sweetheart?"

"Put it on me, Chase. Everyone's waiting for us," I say as I glance around the *Savage Asylum* parking lot where all the original charter members are sitting on their bikes, ready to ride.

With a heavy sigh, Chase finally places the helmet on my head. And then, with shaking fingers, he fastens the chin strap and tightens it.

"Thank you," I tell him, meaning not just for making sure my head is protected but for finally pushing aside his fear to let me ride with him.

He gives me a quick kiss and then grabs his helmet to get himself ready.

Rather than wear a dress, I'm in a black pants suit to make riding easier. I throw a leg over the seat and wait for Chase to join me.

First, he walks over to Torin, who is sitting on his bike. He stayed at the farmhouse with War and the prospects keeping an eye on him yesterday but also giving him space. Chase is trying to do the same, even though he would rather be by his brother's side all day and night.

"You sure you want to ride?" Chase asks Torin. "Turtle can drive you..."

"No," Torin answers. "I need to do this on my bike."

"Okay," Chase says, wrapping him in a back-thumping embrace before he comes back to his bike. "Ready?" he asks me.

I nod even though no one is ever ready to go to a funeral, especially one as difficult as today's.

Finally, Chase climbs on, and I wrap my arms tightly around his waist. He reaches down and grabs my right hand to kiss the top of it and then, flipping it over, kisses his name before putting it back around his waist.

Everyone waits for Torin to crank his bike before they all do the same. Then, their president pulls out first, followed by Chase and then the rest of their brothers in the lot.

There are hundreds of bikes lined up on either side of the strip for at least a mile to show their respects to Torin and Kennedy. The sight sends goosebumps up and down my arms because I've never seen anything like it. All these men, and a few women riding with them, are all hurting too.

The bikes on the street come roaring to life behind us after the original charter passes by. I can feel the rumble of the engines all the way through my soul.

Most riders stay on their bikes when we stop at the cemetery, because that would be too many boots stomping around on graves. There's a white tent set up with several chairs and a garden full of flowers underneath. Kelsey, Kennedy's sister, and her two men are already seated. They stand up to look out at the sea of bikes on the road in awe.

Torin walks up and hugs Kelsey tight before the two of them exchange a few tearful words. And then Torin takes a seat next to her, with Chase on his other side and me holding his hand beside him. The rest of the chairs fill up quickly, and the rest of the men stand behind them as we all face the silver casket in front of us. It remains closed, probably because the sight of the mother holding her child would only make this more difficult.

After the preacher says a few words, each of the members who came to the graveside line up to pick a white rose out of a loose bouquet. Pressing a soft kiss on the petals, they place their rose one at a time on top of the casket.

...

Chase

I KEEP LOOKING over at my brother, waiting for him to lose his shit. Honestly, I don't really know what to expect from a man who has lost his old lady and kid in one fell swoop.

Two days ago, he was tearing down his house. Yesterday, he isolated himself from War and the prospects at the farmhouse. They said they didn't even see his face until this morning before they left for the bar. Torin's like a ticking time bomb that we all know is going to go off; we just don't know when it will happen or what form it will take.

He doesn't say much before the funeral or during it. He simply stares at the casket as if he can't look away. As they begin to lower it into the ground, the spell breaks and Torin jumps to his feet and turns to me.

"When do we ride?" he asks with a clenched jaw.

"As soon as you're ready to go, we'll follow you back to the bar," I tell him as I get to my feet with Sasha's hand still holding mine. I'm still not completely recovered from the tense ride here with her on the back of my bike. We survived, despite how scrambled up my guts feel.

"No, *when* do we ride?" he asks, meaning for Hector.

"Soon," I say, glancing over to Kennedy's sister and men and back to Torin to remind him that we can't talk about that here and now.

"I have to do something," he says.

"I know that," I tell him quietly. "We're meeting when we get back to discuss the details."

"Good," he says. "I won't sleep until I'm putting Hector in one of those caskets."

I nod my agreement, and then Torin strolls off down the grassy hill toward the bikes, barely speaking to anyone along the way.

After saying goodbye to Kelsey, I pull Sasha toward my bike.

"He's gonna be expecting retaliation," she whispers, low enough that only I will hear her. "Hector's not stupid. He'll assume that you all are coming for him."

"I know," I agree, having thought about that myself.

"You should wait until he thinks he's safe and catch him off guard."

"You know we can't do that," I tell her. "Torin wants to go right this second. How am I supposed to convince him to wait while the man who killed his wife and kid is still wandering the streets?"

"I don't know," Sasha says. "Killing him won't bring her back or erase the pain. Torin must know that."

"He does," I agree. "And you're right, ending Hector won't bring Kennedy back or make him forget how much he misses her. But it'll make him think he feels like he did something for her when there's nothing else to be done."

When we reach my bike, I quickly secure Sasha's helmet on her because I know Torin's about to head back.

"We survived the ride here. Think we can try our luck and make it back?" I say, only half joking.

"I told you, baby, our suffering is over. We're gonna be fine," Sasha says.

Since we don't have time to debate that now, I get on my bike and pull away behind Torin as soon as Sasha's arms go around my waist.

While it's terrifying, it also feels pretty damn good having her ride with me again.

CHAPTER THIRTY

Chase

"It's good to see so many of you here and ready to do whatever it takes to seek vengeance for Kennedy," I say to the group around the table and the dozens of men packed in standing. Torin is one of them, refusing to sit in his seat at the table. Several members have noticed, casting curious glances at him and me when neither of us takes the seat at the head of the table.

"While the prudent thing to do may be to sit back and wait for Hector to relax before we hit him, that's not our way. We're gonna go at him savagely tonight, knowing the risks while, at the same time, having the certainty that he won't stand a chance against our show of force."

The guys grunt and cheer their agreement.

"Now, here's our plan," I start. "We'll need our brothers from Virginia to set up a roadblock to the north of Hector's headquarters, Tennessee to the left, and South Carolina to our south, just like the map. Our Emerald Isle charter will come in first from the east, followed by the rest of our forty or so brothers from around our home state who will block up that part of town for us once we're inside. We're gonna hit Hector and his men hard and fast while trying to keep any unarmed women out of the line of fire. Anyone who shoots at you is a target. Roy and Ben from our Charlotte charter will stay here at the clubhouse with Reece who is gonna take out any cameras or recordings in Hector's establishment remotely. For once, we ask that you leave your cuts here in case other cameras see us. Keep your masks on or bandanas around your face at all times, so we can keep track of who the good guys are. Any questions?" I ask.

When there are none, I continue. "Some of us may not come home, some of us may find ourselves wearing orange jumpsuits in new homes. We've got an attorney on speed dial to handle the latter; may your soul rest in peace on the former. You can be assured that the MC will provide for the families of anyone we lose."

"Who's ready to ride?" I ask, and the shouts and yells of so many men is nearly deafening. "We leave in two hours, gentlemen. Until then, gas up, eat your fill, load your guns and fuck your women like it's your last night, because it damn well may be."

With a slam of the gavel, everyone starts filing out of the room as fast as possible. Myself included.

...

Sasha

One second I'm standing in the empty kitchen, and the next, men are pouring in like starving beasts, grabbing anything and everything they can.

"What in the world..." I start. When I step out into the bar, it's

like a freaking orgy. I've never seen so many white asses in my life.
"What's going on?" I ask Maddox, one of the prospects, who is standing in the front of the room, mouth gaping, eyes bulging.

"Beats the fuck out of me, but I can't wait to be a part of it," he replies.

I don't get a chance to respond before my feet leave the floor and then I'm being hauled out the front door.

"Chase?" I yell, to make sure it's his ass I'm looking at.

"Yeah, sweetheart?" the voice I recognize as his, thankfully, asks.

"Where are we going?"

"To my bike."

"Are we going somewhere?" I ask.

"Yeah," he replies. Slapping my ass, he says, "You're going for a ride on my cock."

That sounds good to me. It's pretty dark out already, but there are enough streetlights and members around that it's highly likely someone will see us. At least we won't have to worry about drive-bys. All those bikes from the funeral are parked up and down the street, only leaving enough room for other bikes to get through.

Finally, the world returns to the upright position as Chase sets me down on the back of his bike. He follows, facing me instead of the handlebars.

Throwing my legs over the top of his, I hop up onto his lap and moan when I feel his thick bulge between my legs.

"Is that all for me?" I ask as I wind my arms around his neck.

"Hell yes," he agrees, capturing my lips with his while his hands jerk my shorts down my hips. "Now, pull my cock out so I can give it to you."

Needing him so much I can't wait any longer, I unzip his pants and pull his shaft out while stroking his hot flesh so that I can feel him get even harder in my grip.

Chase pulls at my shorts and panties until he's able to get them off one of my legs; then he grabs my ass cheeks to lift me up in the air.

I line up his cock and lower myself down on it, stretching to take every inch until I can't take any more.

"God, you feel amazing," I tell him as I bury my face in his neck.

"Give me your mouth, sweetheart," he says, so I lean back and let him kiss me, slow and deep, plunging his tongue in and out of my mouth in the same rhythm as he rocks me on his lower body. It's not rough or fast like yesterday. Tonight, Chase is taking his time, savoring every second.

"Someone could see us. It makes this even hotter," I tell him, making him freeze. "What?" I ask.

"You said that the night of the wreck," he points out.

"Well, it's just as true now as it was then. There are a lot of people around," I reply. "But that's okay, baby."

"No, no," he says as she shakes his head. "This is all like déjà vu."

"You brought me out to your bike, remember?" I ask.

"We need to go inside," Chase says.

"What? No. Let's finish what we've already started," I tell him as I run my hands down the sides of his face and buck my hips to remind him he's still inside of me.

"We're leaving in a few hours to go after Hector," he tells me, making my chest burn.

"You are?" I ask.

"This is the only way for you to be safe," Chase says.

"And after he's gone, then you'll find someone else to worry about as a threat. This whole issue is never going to end."

"Yes, it will," he argues. "We'll take out Hector, and everything will go back to the way it was around here."

"Or you could end up in prison or worse..."

"That won't happen," he assures me. "I'll come back to you. Before you wake up in the morning, I'll have my arms around you in bed."

"Everyone is going?" I ask.

"Yes, except for the prospects and Reece. They'll stay here along with two out of towners."

"I've got a bad feeling–" I start to say, but Chase puts his finger to my lips.

"Don't fucking say that," he warns. "This will be easy. There are so many of us that Hector could have an army and we would still take his ass out in a matter of minutes."

Looking at his face, I see how worried he is and know that I don't need to make it worse. He needs me to be supportive. So, I tell him, "Yeah. You're right. Good always wins out over evil, doesn't it?"

"This may be the only situation where we're the good guys," he says. "But yes, we're gonna fucking win."

"Then, if everything is all figured out, why did you stop fucking me?" I ask.

Chase grabs my hips and lifts them high enough to slam me back down on his cock so hard my eyes roll back in my head.

"Keep going," I tell him as I tighten my arms around his neck, holding him as close as possible in case he's wrong.

Actually, I'm almost certain he's wrong and that tonight is gonna be a catastrophe.

But I won't tell Chase that.

Instead, I'll enjoy every second I have with him in case I don't get any more.

CHAPTER THIRTY-ONE

Chase

The highway doesn't feel nearly as peaceful tonight as it usually does. It's a short ride; and with every mile, I second-guess our decision to do this tonight.

I know something's not right when we pull up to Hector's pool hall and it's pitch black, not a single light on. At this time of night, it should be full, like our bar, with people gambling, drinking and getting fucked up on his drugs.

Torin, me and the rest of our crew back our bikes into spots right in front of the building and kill our engines.

"What the fuck do you think he's up to?" I ask Torin.

"No clue," he replies as he looks around with a soldier's eyes searching for the ambush or whatever else Hector has set up for us.

"Maybe the pussy got scared, tucked tail and ran," Abe suggests from his bike that's parked on the other side of mine.

"That doesn't seem like Hector," I reply. "He's after blood. My blood. He wouldn't leave until he hurt me. Reece is supposed to have killed the cameras. Let me call him and see if he spotted anything. Hell, maybe he killed the power to the joint."

The words have barely left my mouth when my phone buzzes in my pocket. As soon as I pull it up and see Maddox's name on the screen, panic grabs me by the throat.

"What's wrong?" I ask.

"The bar's under attack –" he says, and that's all I need to hear before I hang up.

"Back to the bar, now!" I tell the guys before I crank my bike and speed off down the road. And even going as fast as the throttle will let me, it's not fast enough.

When I pull up to the street, I see Ben and Roy, the guys from the Charlotte charter who stayed behind to protect the bar, laid out on the ground next to their bikes. Seeing them, I fucking know that they're dead and that there's not going to be any survivors in the building.

Still, I have to see for myself. With my heart trying to pound its way through my chest, I lay my bike down and race toward the front door with my gun out and raised.

"Chase, wait!" I vaguely hear Torin yell over the roar of engines filling up the parking lot. But I don't stop. I can't even if it's an ambush inside just waiting to blow my head off.

"*Sasha*!" I yell when I step inside and find the bar destroyed, tables turned over, the jukebox on its side, broken bottles of booze everywhere.

Thank fuck there are no more bodies.

Where is everyone? Did they run downstairs for cover when they heard gunfire?

The basement door has dozens of bullet holes in it along with the keypad meant to keep people out, so all I have to do is push it open to go through it. "Sasha!" I yell as I jog down the stairs.

Every apartment door has been busted open and sprayed with bullets, but I don't look inside any of them. Casings cover the floor, along with smears of blood like someone was dragged away. My boots stop just out front of my room, and I have to fight with myself to make me look inside.

With shaking hands, I burst through it...and find it empty.

Where the hell is she?

Fuck! Did they take her and the other girls?

Pulling out my phone, I call her number. The line clicks over, but I don't hear anything.

"Sasha?" I shout.

"Ch- " it sounds like she starts to say my name but her words cut out.

"Sasha, where are you?" I yell as the other guys catch up to me and start looking through all the rooms.

"The whole place is empty," Abe remarks when he appears at my side.

"Where the fuck is everyone?" Torin asks. "War's checking on Roy and Ben, but it doesn't look good. Abe, get on the phone and try to call Maddox again."

"Chase? Chase, I'm here. I'm at the farmhouse," Sasha finally says clearly through the phone line.

"Oh, thank fuck," I reply with a heavy exhale of relief. "Are you okay? Are the girls with you?"

"Yes," she says.

"Good, sweetheart. I'm so fucking glad to hear your voice," I tell her.

"What happened? Are you okay?" she asks frantically.

"No one was at the fucking pool hall!" I explain to her.

"Oh crap! That must be why Reece had Turtle load us all up and bring us here," Sasha tells me.

"Yeah, well it's a damned good thing," I say. "Is he there with you?"

"No," she answers.

"Fuck! What about Maddox and Holden?" I ask.

"No, it's just the girls, me and Turtle. Why?"

"Hector attacked the bar after we left. Ben and Roy, two of our brothers from Charlotte, are most likely dead. I got a call from Maddox and came back, but now we don't know where the hell those three are."

"God, Chase, I'm so sorry," she says. "Do you want us to come back?"

"No, this place is a goddamn mess," I tell her as I look around at the destruction. "Stay there. I'm on my way."

"Okay. I love you," Sasha responds with a sigh.

"Love you too, sweetheart," I say before ending the call.

"What the hell is going on?" Torin asks as he stabs his fingers through his hair. "Are they okay?"

"Yeah, the women are. They're with Sasha at the farmhouse."

All the guys curse in relief, until Abe holds up a hand for silence. "Maddox?" he barks into the phone. "Slow down, kid, I'm gonna put you on the speaker. Chase and Torin are right here too."

Holding the phone out, there's a beep as the speaker clicks on. The sound of ragged breathing echoes from the phone. "You still there?" Maddox asks.

"Yeah, Mad-man, we're here," I yell. "Where the fuck are you?"

"Reece sent the girls off to the farmhouse when Hector's went dark. So then Holden and I were just sitting around the bar when all of a sudden the bastards started shooting up the place. I called you while I was running downstairs to get Reece."

"Are you guys okay?" I bark at the phone, trying to get Maddox to focus. "There's a helluva lot of blood down here."

"It's not ours," Reece's calm, clipped voice says. "Those sons of bitches came out of nowhere."

"Who and how many?" I ask.

"They were definitely Hector's men," Reece mutters. "I've seen them on the video feeds. It was at least half a dozen who rushed inside, maybe more outside. They all made it out, but two of them had to be carried."

"You should have seen him," Maddox yells. "He ran out of his room looking like Rambo or something. This motherfucker had a M60 in his hands!"

"It's a M240," Reece grumbles in irritation.

"Anyway, he lit the place up like Christmas," Maddox cackles. "I followed him up the stairs when they retreated, and we got out. Holden wasn't hurt, he took off out the backdoor. We found him out at the edge of the woods and we're still hunkered down here in the swamp."

"Find your way back to the clubhouse," Torin says at the same time sirens can be heard from upstairs. "Our men from Charlotte are either dead or headed that fucking way."

"Damn," Reece mutters. "I'm sorry. I should've seen them coming..."

"It's not your fault," I tell him. "You're not fucking psychic. There was no way for any of us to know this would happen."

"I had a feeling that motherfucker was up to something when the pool hall emptied out," Reece says. "That's why I sent the girls away. I was hoping the jackass was just running. I hate it when I'm fucking right."

"You did good saving the girls and the prospects," I say. "Now get back here so we can find that bastard and make him pay."

After I end the call, Torin turns to Sax and tells our communications man, "Keep the Carolina charters here and divide up the rest to ride in every possible fucking direction. I want them to look under every single crack whore and drug dealer until we find Hector."

"Yes, sir," Sax says before he runs up the stairs to start making assignments.

"Goddamn him!" Torin roars before he rams his fist into the wall, making plaster dust rain down on all of us.

"We're gonna get him," I promise my brother when I grip his shoulder, pulling him away from the wall before he breaks his hand and can't ride. "The fucker may have got away tonight, but he can't hide forever. We'll find him, no matter how long it takes. And then we'll make him pay. You hear me?" I ask him.

"Yeah," he grumbles as his shoulders slump and his head hangs in defeat.

No, this isn't a defeat, I tell myself. It's just a temporary setback. We may have lost two good men, but Hector's day of reckoning *will* come.

"You gonna be okay here? I need to take some of the boys to pick the girls up from the farmhouse."

"Yeah, this is all going to have to be cleaned up," Torin responds in a flat tone that I don't like. "Hector's destroyed my entire life, and I *swear to fucking Christ, I'm going to clean it up,*" he hisses.

"Most of the crew will stay here to help," I tell him, even though I understand what he really means about cleaning up. "Start here, tonight, just picking up things around the club. It's going to be a big job, but we'll get it done, together."

Torin gives me a sharp nod, then disappears down the hall. I look around at the somber faces of my brothers, gathered in the wreckage of our clubhouse and surrounded by even more death. "Let's go get our girls," I tell them with a sigh.

...

Sasha

As SOON AS I hear the rumble of the motorcycles, I go running out to the front porch.

Chase doesn't waste a second parking his bike and ripping off his helmet before he heads for me. I meet him halfway, jumping into his arms and wrapping mine around his neck to squeeze him tight.

"Are you trying to give me a heart attack?" he asks through panting breaths like he ran all the way here.

"No, I'm sorry I didn't call and let you know where I was, but you had your hands full," I tell him when I finally ease up my hold on his shoulders to pull back and see his face.

"I'm so damn glad you were here and safe," Chase says when his hands come to rest on my hips. "I just can't figure out how we fucked things up tonight."

"It's not your fault," I assure him. "You were going after them, and they were expecting it. I was worried that they might try to hit us again."

"Us," he repeats.

"I meant the MC," I correct.

"It's okay, sweetheart, you're part of the Kings now too," Chase tells me, making me give him a small smile of thanks for that sentiment.

"In that case, there's just one other little question I think the MC needs to worry about right now," I tell him.

"What's that?" he asks with a furrowed brow.

"How did Hector know *when* you guys would show up? Even if he had eyes on you and watched you leave, that wouldn't have been enough time for his guys to evacuate and head an hour up the coast to Emerald Isle."

"What are you saying?" Chase asks as he thinks it over with his forehead creased. Finally, he lowers his voice and says, "You think we have a rat?"

Nodding, I tell him, "Hector *knew* when Kennedy was at the clubhouse. And from what I noticed, she wasn't there often, right? And he also knew when to vanish and hit the bar again. Maybe he just had someone tailing you..."

"No, a rat makes more sense," Chase says with a clenched jaw. "We had the entire strip monitored on camera for a mile each way, and Reece would've noticed someone following Kennedy that day. I'm sure he's been over that footage a dozen times by now."

"Exactly," I agree.

"Great, now we have to find out where the hell Hector is before Torin burns down the entire state looking for him, while there's a rat in our midst, possibly going behind our backs to warn the asshole about our every move," Chase grumbles, low enough that the men and women coming out of the house can't hear him.

"I know," I say quietly. "Just please be careful and make sure Abe always has your back when you ride. You trust him completely, don't you?"

"Fuck, yes. There's no way in hell he's the rat," Chase answers.

"Then he'll help keep you safe for me," I tell him.

Licking his lips as he lowers his eyes in thought, Chase says, "Sweetheart, shit around here is gonna get dangerous for everyone. I know being with me isn't safe for you, and never will be. I can't guarantee I won't get hurt or that you won't either, but I'll try to be smarter and do everything I can to protect you if you decide you want to take a chance on us again."

"Okay," I agree with a smile, glad that it sounds like he's finally going to stop pushing me away out of fear of losing me.

"Okay?" he asks.

"Yes. That's what I want. I told you that I'm well aware of all the risks that come along with you and the MC, and I think you're worth it."

"You're sure?"

"Yes!" I reply adamantly.

"Then, once everything settles down around here, how about we finally take that trip to Vegas?" he asks with a grin.

"Absolutely," I answer without hesitation before I lift my lips to his for a long, sweet kiss. One that I know won't be our last.

EPILOGUE

Sasha
A few days later...

SATURDAY AFTERNOON I'M GOING THROUGH MY HUGE PILE OF clothes that's been tossed on Chase's bed at the farmhouse, hanging each article one at a time in his closet. What may seem like a tedious task to some is as exciting as winning the lottery to me, because it means that Chase and I are moving in together.

While I love the clubhouse, we both thought that it would be nice to have a place to ourselves where we can cook and eat naked in the kitchen if we so choose.

Everything is damn near perfect, including the fact that the news station hasn't uttered a word about firing me even though my affiliation with the MC is out in the open. In fact, I'm pretty sure that's one of the main reason's they've been so nice to me lately. The only thing that still weighs heavily on me is not speaking to my parents for weeks now...

My cell phone beeps from the back pocket of my cutoffs, so I pull it out, hoping it's a message from Chase.

Sure enough, it is. The message is confusing yet thrilling.

Put on a fancy dress, sweetheart, and be ready at the farmhouse at six.

That message is quickly followed up with a correction.

Scratch that. I should've said OUR house.

Grinning like a lunatic, my fingers tap out an instant response.

I'll be ready at OUR house, but where are we going?

Chase's reply is short.

If I told you, it wouldn't be a surprise.

I'm not all that shocked that he would plan something for me, but I am curious about why he wants me to dress "fancy" since Chase doesn't own a single thing formal. I know this because of who he is and the fact that I'm trying to squeeze my clothes into the closet with all the things that he hung up days ago because he was so eager to get moved in. All he owns are jeans, most with holes in them, t-shirts, wife beaters, a few hoodies for winter, and boots. That's it.

Still, I follow his instructions. And after my makeup is done and hair has been arranged with loose curls over my bare shoulders, I pick out a purple and silver sleeveless gown with nearly a billion sequins and a slit that goes all the way up to my thigh. It's the most extravagant dress I own, and I've only worn it once to the AP award banquet last year.

Pairing the dress with silver, strappy heels, I'm ready to go a few minutes before six. I head down the stairs and wait in the living room until I hear the crunch of gravel outside. When I jump up to look out the front window, my jaw falls open at the sight of a long, black limo. Even more shocking than the limo out here in the rural part of town is the tall, handsome, bearded man who climbs out of it in a black tuxedo.

"Oh, my God," I mutter aloud when I finally realize that the man is Chase. He looks so different that it didn't quite register.

Rushing to the front door, I throw it open and say, "Chase, baby, are you feeling okay?"

"I feel great, sweetheart," he replies with a grin. "And you look...

damn, you're sexy as fuck," he adds as his eyes lower and take in every inch of my curves filling out the snug dress. I throw in a slow spin for him to get the full view of my backside too.

"Get your ass down here before I drag you upstairs and all my hard work on your surprise goes down the drain," he grumbles, refusing to come up the stairs to the porch.

That makes me laugh. And while I wouldn't mind if we stayed here and tumbled on the pile of clothes I left up on the bed, I hold on to the railing and walk down the steps toward Chase because I need to see what he's been up to.

"Thank you," I tell him with a quick kiss on his cheek before I run my hands down the lapels of his tux to make sure I'm not seeing things.

"For what?" he asks. "You don't even know what it is yet."

"No, but I'm sure I'll love it," I tell him.

"I'm gonna remind you of those words later," he mutters, making me worry a tad since he sounds so serious.

"Come on," Chase says, before I can question him further. He takes my hand and walks me to the back of the limo, and then opens the door for me to climb in first.

"Wow, this is...wow," I say as I slide across the black leather seat to make room for Chase. He slips in and shuts the door. There's a screen up, so I can't see the driver, but we have the enormous back seat to ourselves that could easily fit about ten normal size people or five of Chase's MC brothers.

"You want something to drink?" Chase asks, nodding to the bar.

"No, I'm okay," I say, now feeling a little nervous about what we're doing.

"Relax, sweetheart," Chase says when he wraps his arm around my shoulders to pull me against him.

I nod, and then try to do as he suggested, inhaling him in, smelling the comforting leather scent of his cut that lingers on him even when he's not wearing it, like it's a part of his skin. God, I love that smell and I love him.

"Any news on Hector?" I ask in the silence.

"Not even so much as one fucking ping," Chase huffs. "Reece has alerts set up for him and his daughter, but so far they haven't used a single credit card to give away their location."

"You'll find him," I say with my hand rubbing his thigh. "How's Torin?"

"Spiraling," he grumbles. "I think he's moved from the anger stage of grief to the depressed one. He's drinking way too much. This morning I found him passed out asleep on the stairs of the bar when I went in. I asked the guys why no one fucking moved him to a bed, and they all said Torin fought them off and told them he, quote, 'didn't deserve any such comforts.'"

"Jesus," I reply with a sigh. "I'm sorry," I tell Chase, covering the top of his hand to give it a squeeze.

"I don't know what the fuck to do for him," he admits.

"Give him his space to grieve until you find the asshole who hurt him so that he can finally get his vengeance," I suggest.

"Yeah, well I can't believe my brother didn't snap sooner, before all of this shit. Sax and I are trying to handle all the club's legit businesses, and we're both drowning. I don't know how Torin did it all on his own."

"You'll figure it out until he's ready to take over again," I assure him.

"I hope so," Chase responds with a sigh. "But enough of the heavy shit. This is supposed to be a good night for you." He turns his head to look out the window and says, "We're here."

I hadn't been paying attention to where we were going, so I'm stunned when I look out my window and see the nondescript, three-story brick building with a flag pole out front. We're at West Carteret High School - *our* old high school.

"What are we doing here?" I ask Chase since it's a Saturday and the school is, of course, closed with summer break right around the corner.

"Let's go and I'll show you," he says with a quick kiss on my lips before he gets out of the limo and offers me his hand. I take it and let him pull me to my feet.

"I haven't been back here since before the accident," I admit to him as I take a deep breath in and let it out, remembering all the good times and bad. Mostly good ones with Chase, making out or doing more in the parking lot; stealing kisses in the hallways; working on my dad's Mustang in shop class...

"This way," Chase says, taking my hand and leading us toward the building back to the left – the gymnasium.

"You should've had me wear my gym uniform instead of the fancy dress," I tell Chase as he pulls on the handle of the front door and it opens. "Why is it unlocked? Are we trespassing?" I ask when my heart begins to race with excitement.

"Believe it or not, we're not trespassing. The principal opened it for me after I made a big donation," he answers with a smirk over his shoulder as he hauls me inside the pitch-black building.

Or it was completely dark until the gym door slams shut behind us. Then, it's like a switch is flipped and the whole place lights up like Christmas. There are strings of white lights hanging everywhere, including on the trees and tables that have been set up. A disco ball hangs over what looks like a dance floor, throwing off bright colors.

"It's beautiful," I tell Chase as my eyes start to go blurry from the tears clouding them.

"It's prom," he says, and that's all it takes to cause the tears to overflow down my cheeks. "I'm sorry we missed ours, sweetheart."

"You..." I start, but my throat feels like it's closed shut, so I smack Chase's chest instead.

"Last night was the school's prom, so I had them keep up the decorations. You said you regretted missing ours..." he replies as he rapidly blinks his fern-green eyes and looks away like he's tearing up too.

My man may be an outlaw biker in the Savage Kings MC, but he can still be romantic and sensitive too, making me love him even more.

"Thank you," I tell him when I throw my arms around his neck to hold him. His arms wind around my waist; and then, as if on cue, music starts to play, a slow song.

"The prospects are in charge of operating the lights and DJ'ing," Chase informs me as we begin to sway to the tune. "They'll keep their mouths shut, while I'm guessing my brothers would've never let me live this down."

"Then they need to learn how to treat a woman like a queen," I whisper in his ear. "And your brothers will be so jealous when they hear about how you get rewarded for this. I'm thinking your dick may be spending more time in my mouth than it does in your pants."

"Is that right?" Chase asks when he pulls his face back to look at me with a grin.

"Yep," I reply.

"Well then, in that case, I can't fucking wait to see what you'll do for this," he tells me before he removes his hand from me. My lovesick brain is still trying to process everything when Chase pulls out a small black box from his pocket. Opening it up to reveal a huge diamond solitaire, he says, "I should've given you a ring like this years ago. Will you wear it and be my old lady no matter what obstacles come between us?"

"Yes," I tell him, but it comes out softly, so I say it again, "Yes, Chase! Yes, baby," I repeat before I grab the sides of his face to join our lips.

Chase returns the kiss for a moment before breaking it to remove the ring from the box. Reaching for my left hand, he slips the diamond onto my finger.

"There, now you can't change your mind," he says, bringing my knuckles to his lips to kiss them.

"I won't change my mind," I assure him.

"Remember you said that," Chase says. "Because I asked your parents to come here too."

"You did *what*?" I exclaim as my neck snaps around the gymnasium, looking for them. I finally spot them over near the entrance where it's the darkest. "Are you kidding me?" I ask Chase. "Why? Why would you do that? They hurt us both for years!"

"I know," he says as he takes both of my hands in his and dips his head down to hold my gaze. "What they did was fucked up, and I absolutely hate it; but at the same time, I know what it's like to be without you. I want you to just consider letting them be a part of your life again. It's okay to be angry at them. I am too. I just don't want you to regret pushing them away in a few years if you lose them. Life's too short, sweetheart."

My anger quickly melts away as Chase's words sink in. Of all the people who should want to steer clear of my parents, he's not only trying to forgive them but urging me to do the same. God, I'm so lucky to have this man in my life again.

"I love you," I tell him with my chin trembling from emotion when I grab his lapels.

"I love you too," he replies with a grin. "So fucking much."

The End

ALSO BY LANE HART AND D.B. WEST

CATCH UP WITH CHASE AND SASHA IN ABE'S BOOK WHEN THEY FINALLY GET THEIR VEGAS WEDDING!

FIND OUT MORE ABOUT ABE HERE AND START READING!

ABOUT THE AUTHORS

New York Times bestselling author Lane Hart and husband D.B. West were both born and raised in North Carolina. They still live in the south with their two daughters and enjoy spending the summers on the beach and watching football in the fall.

Connect with D.B.:
Twitter: https://twitter.com/AuthorDBWest
Facebook: https://www.facebook.com/authordbwest/
Website: https://www.dbwestbooks.com
Email: dbwestauthor@outlook.com

Connect with Lane:
Twitter: https://twitter.com/WritingfromHart
Facebook: http://www.facebook.com/lanehartbooks
Instagram: https://www.instagram.com/authorlanehart/
Website: http://www.lanehartbooks.com
Email: lane.hart@hotmail.com

Join Lane's Facebook group to read books before they're released, help choose covers, character names, and titles of books! https://www.facebook.com/groups/bookboyfriendswanted/

Find all of Lane's books on her Amazon author page!

Sign up for Lane's newsletter to get updates on new releases and freebies!

Printed in Great Britain
by Amazon

43286948R00136